TIDES OF DECEPTION

LANTERN BEACH ROMANTIC SUSPENSE, BOOK 1.

CHRISTY BARRITT

River Heights

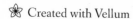

COMPLETE BOOK LIST

SQUEAKY CLEAN MYSTERIES:

- #1 Hazardous Duty
- #2 Suspicious Minds
- #2.5 It Came Upon a Midnight Crime (novella)
- #3 Organized Grime
- #4 Dirty Deeds
- #5 The Scum of All Fears
- #6 To Love, Honor and Perish
- #7 Mucky Streak
- #8 Foul Play
- #9 Broom & Gloom
- #10 Dust and Obey
- #11 Thrill Squeaker
- #11.5 Swept Away (novella)
- #12 Cunning Attractions

#6 Flaw Abiding Citizen

#7 Gaffe Out Loud (coming soon)

#8 Joke and Dagger (coming soon)

Raven Remington

Relentless 1

Relentless 2 (coming soon)

Holly Anna Paladin Mysteries:

#1 Random Acts of Murder

#2 Random Acts of Deceit

#2.5 Random Acts of Scrooge

#3 Random Acts of Malice

#4 Random Acts of Greed

#5 Random Acts of Fraud

#6 Random Acts of Iniquity (coming soon)

#7 Random Acts of Outrage (coming soon)

Lantern Beach Mysteries

#1 Hidden Currents

#2 Flood Watch

#3 Storm Surge

#4 Dangerous Waters

#5 Perilous Riptide

#6 Deadly Undertow

Lantern Beach Romantic Suspense

Tides of Deception

Shadow of Intrigue (coming soon)

Storm of Doubt (coming soon)

Carolina Moon Series:

Home Before Dark

Gone By Dark

Wait Until Dark

Light the Dark

Taken By Dark

Suburban Sleuth Mysteries:

Death of the Couch Potato's Wife

Cape Thomas Series:

Dubiosity

Disillusioned

Distorted

Standalone Romantic Mystery:

The Good Girl

Suspense:

Imperfect

The Wrecking

Standalone Romantic-Suspense:

Keeping Guard

The Last Target

Race Against Time

Ricochet

Key Witness

Lifeline

High-Stakes Holiday Reunion

Desperate Measures

Hidden Agenda

Mountain Hideaway

Dark Harbor

Shadow of Suspicion

The Baby Assignment

Nonfiction:

Characters in the Kitchen

Changed: True Stories of Finding God through Christian Music (out of print)

The Novel in Me: The Beginner's Guide to Writing and Publishing a Novel (out of print)

CHAPTER ONE

"I UNDERSTAND," Austin Brooks muttered into his phone. "You've given me a lot to think about, and I'll wait for a follow-up call."

Austin hit End on his cell, trying to come to terms with what he'd just learned. But his thoughts staggered inside him, tumultuous and unsettled instead.

He'd just gotten the call he'd been waiting for. So why did unease and regret tug at him? He'd set all of this in motion, so none of it should be a surprise.

This wasn't the time to chew on those thoughts, though. No, his current job needed all his attention.

Austin put the four-wheel-drive vehicle back into Drive. He adjusted his grip on the steering wheel, pushed his sunglasses up higher, and glanced out the window.

The ocean stared back, and it looked as unsettled as

his thoughts. Then again, the water always looked angry on Lantern Beach. People didn't call this area of the East Coast the Graveyard of the Atlantic for nothing.

"Was that an update on your secret project?" Skye Lavinia's voice pulled him from his thoughts.

Austin glanced over at her. He'd temporarily forgotten she was on beach-patrol duty with him. Two of the regular rescue crew had gotten food poisoning at a party the night before, and Austin had been called in as a last-minute replacement.

He'd just been recertified, but it had been a long time since he'd lifeguarded. With the influx of crowds they'd had here in Lantern Beach during the off-season, everyone was short-staffed—including beach rescue. Skye was just along for moral support.

His heart skipped a beat when he saw her lithe frame —as it always did when he looked at her.

She was beautiful.

And off-limits.

The walls she kept up around her made that clear, and Austin would be wise to keep it in mind.

He remembered her question, and his phone call echoed in his mind. "Yes, that was about my secret project."

Austin turned back to scan the beachgoers in front of him for a moment. Though it was October, there were still people here on the shores soaking in the unseasonably warm day.

"When are you going to tell me what you're doing?"

Austin shrugged, partly enjoying her interest in his project, and, in return, her interest in him. He probably enjoyed it more than he should. But Austin wasn't being coy as much as he was cautious when it came to keeping her at arm's length.

"I don't know when I'll spill the beans," he finally said as they bounced over the uneven sand. "Maybe I'll tell *you* what I'm doing as soon as you tell *me* a secret—like why you hate the water so much."

The curiosity slipped from her eyes, and Skye raised her chin teasingly. "By the way, watch out for that lady with the earbuds on. I'm sure she doesn't hear you coming. And, I see you how you are, but I'm not making any deals. We can both just keep our secrets."

And maybe that was their problem. There were too many secrets between them.

Besides, calling it a secret project made the whole thing sound so lighthearted—like Austin was building a bookshelf or starting his own YouTube channel for his woodworking endeavors. But the truth was, Austin's undertaking was really a lot more personal.

And maybe that's what really stopped him from sharing any details with Skye. It would be like sharing a piece of his heart. Once that piece was gone, he might never get it back.

Focus, Austin. Focus. And why are you mentally quoting after-school specials from your childhood?

He grabbed a handful of chocolate-covered raisins from the bag beside him and popped them in his mouth as he skirted around a group of fishermen who chatted while their rods rested in holders in the sand.

No sooner had Austin gone around them did something catch his eye. He pressed the brakes as he spotted something in the water a good twenty yards out. He squinted. Were those hands? Flailing hands?

"What is it?" Concern gripped Skye's features as she leaned toward him.

His heartrate quickened. He jammed the truck in Park, threw his door open, and his feet hit the sand.

"I think there's someone out there in the water." Austin stared at the ocean and squinted when he saw the person again. Someone definitely needed help out there. "Do me a favor—call backup."

Wasting no more time, he stripped off his shirt and grabbed the orange rescue tube from the pickup bed and strapped it across his chest. He abandoned his flip-flops and dashed toward the water.

Maybe the ominous feeling in his gut wasn't a fluke.

Skye held her breath as she watched Austin dive into the turbulent ocean. She watched his strong, powerful strokes as he went against the current, putting his own life on the line to save another. As he battled the waves, her gaze darted beyond Austin. Someone *was* out there—and in trouble.

Oh, Lord, please protect Austin. And protect the person he's trying to save. Don't let the ocean claim an innocent life.

She called for backup. Then, moving in autopilot, she climbed from the beach patrol truck and lumbered toward the raging shoreline. As the wind blew against Skye's face, she raked a hand through her hair, trying to get the strands from her eyes so she could watch the scene unfold.

A small crowd gathered, each person's gaze fixated on the rescue. The beach activities around her seemed to stop—the volleyball game, the boogie boarding, the fishing. Everyone waited to see what would happen.

Skye wrapped her arms across her chest and continued to stare, trying not to anticipate the worst. The ocean was a formidable foe. Skye shuddered whenever she thought about going in those waters.

She wasn't a strong swimmer—and she'd almost lost her life to the ocean once. Ever since then, her throat went dry whenever anyone suggested she go deeper than to her knees in the water.

She pushed aside the memories.

Instead, her heart went into her throat as she waited, as she watched. Austin reached the person and wrapped his arms around the guy's chest, the rescue tube between them. Then, on his back, Austin began swimming toward the shore.

Skye released her breath. Maybe this would all be okay. But Austin still had to make it back to dry land. The waves and the current were strong today, and the swim would be exhausting, even for the most seasoned rescuer.

Dear Lord, watch over them. Please.

Just as paramedics pulled up and rushed toward the crowds, Austin reached the shore. He stood, reached into the water, and carried the victim toward the sand.

The victim was . . . a boy.

That had been a *boy* out there, Skye realized. The child was probably only seven or eight years old, at the most.

Austin placed him on the sand, and the paramedics surrounded the boy, taking over. Skye moved through the crowds until she reached Austin. She studied him for any sign he'd been harmed.

His dark, wavy hair was wet and shoved back from his face. Specks of water still clung to his short, neat beard.

He had the hard-earned physique of someone who did both physical labor and took care of himself.

And he appeared to be okay right now.

"You good?" Skye gently touched his arm, wanting to hear the words for herself.

He nodded, still hauling in deep breaths. "Yeah, I'm fine."

"Good job out there." She'd always known he was a hero, but today had only confirmed it.

Austin's gaze didn't leave the boy. "I'm just glad I got to him in time."

The boy . . . he was conscious. Coughing. Lying on the sand.

At least he was awake and breathing.

Thank You, Jesus.

Skye glanced around the windswept landscape. Where were this boy's parents? Why weren't they out here? Worried about him?

Her gaze veered back to the boy. She sucked in a breath when she saw his face. His dark hair. His high cheek bones. The broad set of his eyebrows.

Somehow . . . some reason . . . he looked familiar.

But that was crazy. Unless maybe the boy and his family had come to her produce stand earlier this week. That was probably it.

Yet, if Skye had seen him earlier, she would remember.

His familiarity wasn't because she'd seen him before. It was because—

Before the thought could fully form, a cry cut through the crowds behind her. A woman split the sea of onlookers and emerged with her arms outstretched. She dropped to the ground beside the boy, sobbing as she leaned toward him.

"My baby . . . my baby . . . Is he okay?"

Skye could see only the back of the woman's head, a bob of big, dark curls that stopped at the woman's shoulders. A silky housecoat with teal and pink flowers draped her slim figure. Something about her screamed affluent and pampered.

Was this the boy's mom? Where had she come from?

Skye glanced behind her. Maybe she'd been at one of the huge mansions on this part of the beach. This stretch of houses was known by locals as Ritzy Row. They were the rental homes that featured ten bedrooms, extravagant pools, and a couple even had lazy rivers.

The rentals cost big bucks.

As in, twelve-thousand-dollars-a-week big bucks.

Skye did a double take when she saw movement across the dunes. A man and a woman rushed over a wooden boardwalk, past a gazebo, and hit the sand.

Urgency tinged their steps and movements as they darted toward the scene.

Everything else seemed to fade as Skye watched them.

No, it couldn't be . . .

She swung her gaze back toward the woman leaning over the boy. Then she swerved back toward the couple. Fact collided with emotion in Skye's head until her lungs squeezed.

"Skye?"

She glanced over. Austin lightly touched her arm as he peered at her inquisitively. At some point, he'd pulled a shirt on. Spray from the waves misted his skin.

"Are you okay?" He squinted, still studying her with obvious worry. "You look pale."

She barely heard him. Instead, she turned back to the scene, to where the couple now cut through the crowds, and joined the woman and the boy.

The couple . . . the man with his expensive khaki shorts, boat shoes, and a polo. The woman with blonde hair, set with enough hairspray that it could withstand even this wind, and wearing a dress and pearls.

Pearls . . .

It couldn't be. But it was. That necklace confirmed it.

This couple was Atticus and Ginger Winthrop.

The last time Skye had seen them had been on the worst day of her life.

As the memories rushed back to her, everything blurred around Skye. A part of her life she'd tried to forget roared to the surface, and despair bit as hard and deep as if a shark had clutched her in its teeth and dragged her under.

CHAPTER TWO

AUSTIN CAUGHT Skye before she withered to the sand.

Her eyes fluttered open as she sagged against him, but the same shell-shocked look remained on her face. What had just happened? A surge of worry rushed through him.

"Skye, are you okay?" He studied her face for a sign of what was going on. He'd never seen her look like this before.

She straightened and nodded, but the motion was faint and unconvincing. Her gaze went back to the group gathered around the boy. Her mind was here, yet it seemed to be in another world as well.

"I'm . . . fine," she finally said.

"Skye . . ." Austin desperately wished the woman would open up to him, that she would stop remaining at a distance. But there was something in her, holding her back every time she started to get close.

Like right now. It was like Skye didn't hear him. Instead, she stepped toward the boy, her gaze fastened on the scene, and a million unsaid things stretching between the two of them.

Austin didn't push. Instead, he watched the paramedics work on the boy and prayed he'd be okay.

The ocean had been even more fierce than usual, and the swim had taken all of Austin's strength. His heart still pounded. The breeze hit his wet skin, causing bumps to ripple across his arms.

"Hey, guys. I heard through dispatch we had a rescue. You okay?"

Austin looked over and saw Cassidy Chambers, the new police chief in town and his best friend's wife. She strode toward them, the wind tugging her blonde hair from its bun. She pivoted toward the scene, obviously only pausing by Austin and Skye long enough to check on them.

Austin nodded. "I think he'll be okay too."

"Did he get caught in a rip current?" Cassidy glanced over as paramedics slipped an oxygen mask on the boy.

"No idea. His parents didn't get here until after I rescued the boy. I'm not sure of the details."

Cassidy's eyebrows flickered up. "I'll reserve my judgment until I hear their side of the story."

Austin ran a hand through his wet, salty hair and remembered just how strong the currents had been out there. They'd been more than strong—they'd been deadly. Red flags were flying across the beach, signaling that vacationers should stay out of the water for their safety. Why hadn't this boy's parents been supervising him?

"He shouldn't have been out in this water," Austin said. "That's for sure."

"Good work out there," Cassidy said, before continuing to the scene.

The woman was the total opposite of the town's last police chief, Alan Bozeman. Cassidy was competent, she cared about people, and she didn't let anything slip past her. When Bozeman had left, one of his officers—Quinton—had stayed. But the other one had taken a new position in another town. Cassidy was shorthanded until she found someone else to hire.

Austin's gaze went back to Skye. She still watched the scene, almost like a tragedy was playing out in front of her. She'd seen other rescues here on the island. Anyone who'd lived on Lantern Beach for long had. So what was it about this one that had Skye's attention? That made her go pale? Was it because a little boy was involved? Incidents with children were always the worst.

Paramedics put the boy on a stretcher. They would take him to the town's clinic to monitor his vitals. The three people who'd surrounded him—family, Austin assumed—followed after the rescue crew.

A couple minutes later, just as the crowds started to disperse, someone else jogged onto the scene.

Skye sucked in a breath and wobbled beside him. Austin slipped an arm around her waist, just in case her legs turned to jelly again. She didn't push him away. She seemed too focused on the man who'd just shown up.

The man swung around, as if looking for the boy, before his gaze zeroed in on Cassidy. He darted toward her.

"You rescued a boy?" he rushed. "Is he okay? Where is he?"

"He appears to be fine," Cassidy said. "Are you family?"

"Yes, I am. Where did he go? Are you sure he's okay?"

"He's on the way to the town clinic," Cassidy said. "Your other family members are with him."

The man's shoulders sagged with relief. "Thank you. I'll meet them there."

He turned to leave, but his gaze stopped on Skye. His blue eyes widened, and he detoured from his departure and jogged toward her instead.

"Skye?" The man's voice was tinged with disbelief and familiarity. "Is that you?"

Skye stiffened beside him. "Ian . . . it's been a long time."

"Eight years."

Wait . . . these two knew each other? A friendship seemed unlikely between someone free-spirited like Skye and someone who was obviously privileged like Ian. Austin was making a judgment. He knew he was. But Skye hated people who put up pretenses and acted better than others.

Skye glanced over at Austin, seeming to remember his presence, and she nearly startled when her eyes met his. "Austin, this is Ian. Ian, Austin. Ian is . . . an old friend."

Austin didn't bother to extend his hand. Instead, the two men almost seemed to size each other up.

"How long are you here?" Skye asked, not seeming to notice the tension.

"Two weeks," Ian said. "The family . . . well, we have a lot going on. We figured Lantern Beach would be the perfect place to get away and not run into anyone we knew."

"Surprise." Skye's words lacked enthusiasm.

"A good surprise. We should get together and catch up while I'm here. How about tonight? Can we do dinner?"

Say no, Austin mentally pleaded. He didn't like the idea of anyone else being with Skye. Mostly because he wanted her for himself.

Skye hesitated before nodding. "Yeah, let's do that."

Disappointment bit Austin, but he tried not to show it. Skye was a grown woman and could make her own choices.

"Great," Ian said. "I've got to get to the clinic. That was my nephew out there."

"Your nephew?" Skye's voice sounded unusually squeaky.

"Yeah, he slipped out of the house, I guess. He's been chomping at the bit all day today to play in the water. I'm just glad he's okay. I came as soon as I heard."

"The clinic is just down the road," Skye said.

Ian took a step away and paused there on the sand. "How can I find you later?"

"I run the produce stand down the street. It's the only one on the island. Can't miss it."

"Yeah, I saw that on the way in. I'll pick you up there. At seven?"

Skye nodded, but the action was marred with tension. "I'll see you then."

Austin's jaw tightened. Dinner? He hated the idea of it. But as much as he might not like it, Skye was single and free to do what she wanted.

Austin had only hoped that what she wanted was him.

Skye's chest ached as she watched Ian stride across the beach.

Why did he have to show up here of all places? In Lantern Beach? Of all the islands in the United States—in the world—he and his family had chosen this one?

"Skye?"

Austin touched her elbow again and jerked her from her thoughts. Her gaze wandered up to his, and she saw the questions in his eyes.

Did he think . . . did he think she was meeting Ian for a romantic get-together? Because nothing could be further from the truth. Skye didn't want anything to do with Ian Winthrop.

She couldn't spill her motives to Austin. It was too risky, and she feared leading him on. Feared opening up and making herself vulnerable.

Yet her heart wanted nothing more than to abandon all her anxieties and failures and explore what life would be like by Austin's side.

Life by his side would be wonderful. She knew that.

But as soon as Austin learned about her past . . . he

would change his mind about her.

Skye had known from the moment she met Austin that he deserved someone who was wholesome and innocuous.

That person wasn't Skye. Not by any stretch of the imagination. Even though she knew God's grace had made her a new person, not everyone would view her as God did. Nor did God's grace exclude her from the penalties of her actions. Her decisions had consequences.

She swallowed hard and tried to formulate a response to the curiosity in Austin's gaze. Her eyes met his, and Skye shoved the wind-driven hair from her eyes. "I'm sorry. I just feel like . . ."

"You've seen a ghost?"

She nodded, a bit unnerved at how easily the man could read her. "Yeah, like I've seen a ghost."

His gaze flickered in the distance to where Ian had disappeared. "I take it that guy was more than a friend."

How did Skye even answer that? The strong breeze gave her a good excuse to look away, to gather her thoughts, however briefly. "It's . . . complicated."

"I'm sure it is." Austin's voice sounded stiff.

Skye stole another glance at him. She wanted to put her hand on his chest. To explain everything. To somehow erase the multi-layered emotions in Austin's eyes.

Jealousy? She wasn't sure. But maybe something close

to that.

Concern? Definitely.

Curiosity? No doubt.

She snapped back to her senses, realizing this wasn't the time or place to have this conversation. There were too many people. She felt too much pressure—even if it was all internal.

"Listen, I should go," she started. "I need to check with my suppliers on a delivery of greens, and I know you need to keep patrolling the beach."

His jaw stiffened. "You want me to drop you off?"

Skye shook her head, appreciating his offer but needing some time alone. "No, I'll walk. I need to clear my head. But thank you."

"If you insist." Austin started to reach for her but stopped and dropped his hand. "By the way, thanks for keeping me company earlier."

"My pleasure." Skye licked her dry lips. "We'll talk later, okay?"

"Later."

Right now, her thoughts were so tumultuous that she could hardly think. Because that boy she'd seen looked familiar. In fact, he looked like Skye.

But she'd given her baby up for adoption. Ian's family had helped.

Yet what if there was more to that story?

CHAPTER THREE

SKYE LOOKED at herself in the small mirror over her mini bathroom sink one more time and frowned.

What was she thinking agreeing to meet Ian tonight? She should have told him no. But how could she? Especially when she wanted answers so badly. She had to know who that boy was. When she had some answers, maybe she could put to rest all the questions stabbing at her mind.

She turned away from her reflection, grabbed her purse and stepped out of the small RV she called home. It was a retro trailer, white with a teal stripe running down the side. Inside was enough space for a bed, mini-kitchen, and a dining room table that converted into a couch.

Skye had worked hard to make the place her own. She'd used stencils to put a black-and-white chevron design on the old vinyl floor. She'd painted the kitchen cabinets sea-glass blue, had created her own artwork from shells she'd found at the beach, and she'd stitched a quilt from fabric she'd purchased at a thrift store.

What would Ian think if he saw her home? He'd pity her, most likely. Living in a place like this screamed no social affluence.

And that was just one more reason why they could never be together. She liked this simple life she was living.

She climbed on an old, faded beach cruiser that she used sometimes to go back and forth to work and around the island. It was an easier and more cost-efficient way to travel these narrow, crowded roads, especially in the summer when one left turn could cause a ten-minute backup on the two-lane road.

The island was an old fishing community that had transformed into a tourist destination a few decades earlier. People came here for the isolation—and it didn't get much more isolated than this place. From the Outer Banks of North Carolina, visitors had to take a ferry from Hatteras Island to Ocracoke. From Ocracoke Island, they caught another ferry here.

No one came to Lantern Beach by accident. No, the trip required planning and time and a whole lot of patience.

It was one of the reasons Skye had thought the island would be the perfect place to start a new life.

Ten minutes later, Skye spotted Happy Hippy Produce, the fruit and vegetable stand that was her lifeblood. She'd bought an old Chevy van, painted it turquoise also—her favorite color—and she'd had Austin build a pergola for it.

That was the first time the two of them had met, and she'd been smitten with the man from the start. Austin was so sure of himself—something she desperately lacked in herself. Nothing ever frazzled him.

He'd dated other women since they'd known each other, but Skye was certain he wasn't a player. No, if Austin didn't think a relationship would work, he'd cut the girl loose. Skye thought it was pretty respectable.

After Skye's stand had opened, Austin had become a regular. Eventually, he'd invited her to Bible study and really helped change her life for the better. She wasn't where she wanted to be, spiritually speaking, but she wasn't anywhere near where she'd once been.

Over the past several months, Austin had become a great friend. He was always there for her, always patient, and he never pressured her to be someone she wasn't.

When Skye coasted up to the stand on her bike, she studied the black Mercedes there. She pressed on her pedals to slow down before coming to a stop. Ian stepped out of his car and leaned against it with his arms crossed, wearing some blue shorts and a lush-looking pink T-shirt.

"Well, aren't you a sight?" Ian smiled, his eyes showing his approval.

Skye knew she looked like the epitome of a beach girl. She didn't try. It was just that this area and lifestyle agreed with her. The loose hair, sun-kissed cheeks in lieu of makeup, and casual clothing fit her personality to a T. She just hadn't realized it until she'd come here and traded in her black clothes and heavy eyeliner for the all-natural look.

Skye parked her bike behind the stand and joined him. A rush of nerves hit her. "I can't believe you're here, Ian."

Her heart didn't stammer when she saw him like it used to. No, her relationship with Ian all those years ago had thrived on risk and rebellion. That wasn't who she was anymore. But the man still had killer blue eyes that would melt any woman's heart. Even though he was only five foot nine and lean, he carried himself like a giant— just as his father had taught him.

"And I can't believe you're here." He ran his gaze over her again without apology, still smiling with satisfaction. "It's good to see you. Really good."

Skye shoved a lock of hair behind her ear. His compliments didn't affect her anymore. No, she knew Ian's character. He knew how to say just the right things to get what he wanted.

"Maybe we should go eat?" she suggested.

"Yes, let's do that. You mind if I drive? I don't think there's room for both of us on your bike—unless you want to ride on the handlebars."

"That would never work. You'd be the one riding on the handlebars."

He laughed like he liked that idea. "You always did have that wicked sense of humor."

"You can drive." Despite her words, Skye hesitated for just a moment before climbing into his car. Something about getting into a vehicle with Ian felt unnerving, as if she might be traveling back in time.

Her thoughts went to Austin. She should have invited him to come.

But that would be awkward. And unnecessary. Skye could talk to Ian right now without the sort of security Austin brought with him. She just hadn't realized how much she'd come to depend on it.

The inside of Ian's vehicle smelled just like Skye expected it to. Like leather and expensive aftershave. Fancy water bottles littered the floor in the back, along with valet ticket stubs, and a couple parking tickets—even one from here in Lantern Beach.

"Anywhere you recommend around here?" Ian asked, pulling away a little too fast. Gravel flew behind them.

"I'm surprised you haven't tried all the restaurants already."

"We brought Francois with us. He's our cook."

"You have a cook named Francois?" She cast a disbelieving glance his way.

Ian smiled. "Well, his name is actually Frank, but I call him Francois because I think it fits him more."

Skye should have figured. "I see. Let's eat at the Crazy Chefette."

She was certain the place wasn't up to Ian's standards, but she liked it there. Her friend Lisa Garth owned the restaurant, and she came up with insane food combinations that surprised the taste buds in a good way.

Part of Skye didn't want to go there—didn't want to run into Lisa and see the questions in her eyes. The other part of her wanted the security of the familiar. And the Crazy Chefette was definitely familiar.

She only hoped the rest of her friends weren't there, and, if they were, that they didn't try to interfere. No, this dinner would be awkward enough without any of them trying to figure out who Ian was.

She gave Ian directions, and they pulled up to the restaurant a few minutes later. Since it was the off-season, they were seated right away. Lisa spotted her as soon as they took their seats and made her way over to them.

The petite blonde wore her signature lab coat and, as usual, it was splattered with food from her kitchen lab creations, as she called them. "Welcome!"

Lisa's gaze fell on Ian, and a knot formed between her eyes. It was only there a second before her smile widened again. She gave Skye a questioning look, making it clear they needed to talk later.

"If you're not sure what to order, I have this fantastic new meatloaf I made," Lisa started. "It sounds weird, but it has ground chicken, Gouda, and apples. I serve it with a warm kale salad and jicama fries. What do you say?"

Ian's lips turned down in a slight frown. "I'll just start with a lemonade, please."

"Would you like to try my peach lemonade with jalapeño?" Lisa batted her eyelashes—not in a fake way. No, she just got so excited over her edible creations.

"Do you just have regular lemonade?"

Lisa nodded. "I do. I also have a pickle slushy that's to die for."

Ian's frown deepened. "Just regular lemonade would be great."

"I'll take a water," Skye said.

As soon as Lisa walked away, Ian gave Skye a look that

clearly showed he thought Lisa was nuts. "Interesting place."

Skye's defenses rose. Lisa was one of the nicest people Skye knew. "The food is really good. I promise. You'll never forget eating here."

"I bet I won't." He let out a chuckle.

They stared at each other a moment, and that's when Skye felt the awkwardness set in—the awkwardness of lost years. Of having nothing in common anymore. Of being two different people. Of unspoken questions.

Maybe this meeting was a bad idea.

"Here are your drinks," Lisa announced, making it back to their table in record time. She made no effort to leave. No, she took their orders, and, when she was done, her gaze turned to Ian. "So, where are you from?"

"Charlotte."

"I see. You just here for the week?"

"A couple weeks, actually."

She flashed a smile. "Well, I hope you enjoy yourself. Your food will be right out."

After she walked away, Ian started a lighthearted banter. As he always did. He always could make a good first impression.

Their food came only ten minutes later. Skye had ordered the meatloaf—mostly out of loyalty. As much as possible, she tried to stick to a plant-based diet. But she felt the need to support her friend. Ian had ordered the steamer basket with shrimp, cabbage, and onions.

That was when Skye felt like the conversation could really begin.

Because Skye knew she had important things to talk about.

And she couldn't put it off any longer.

CHAPTER FOUR

"HOW'S YOUR NEPHEW?" Skye started, picturing the boy again.

His image had haunted her thoughts since she'd seen him. Skye's paranoia collided with logic. Just because the boy resembled her, that didn't mean he was hers. After all, why would Ian's family keep her baby and tell her the boy had been adopted?

She picked at her meatloaf.

It wouldn't make sense. The Winthrops had made it clear that neither Skye nor Ian were in a good position to take care of a baby. That there were many other families out there who desperately wanted a child. That she was doing the right thing by giving her child to a family in a better position to provide for him.

Ian put down his lemonade and leaned back in his seat. "Briar? He's fine. Thankfully."

Skye tried a bite of jicama fries, but she'd lost her appetite. "What happened? He was really far out in the ocean. I have to admit that I was a little scared for him."

Ian looked across the restaurant a moment before shrugging. "We told Briar not to leave the house, but he did. He thought he could take a swim and be back before we realized it. It was a good thing your friend saw him. In fact, my parents told me to express their thanks."

"You told them I was here in Lantern Beach?" For some reason, the thought made Skye's back muscles—and her lungs—tighten.

"I did. Of course. Why wouldn't I?"

"Your parents were never my biggest fans." No, the couple had gone out of their way to let Skye know she wasn't good enough for their precious, privileged son.

Ian waved her statement off. "You know how they are. No one is good enough for them. Don't take it personally."

"They seem to be doing well." She took a long sip of her water, knowing there was no need to argue. He'd never agree with her.

"They're working hard. Involved in the community. Loving life."

"Any thoughts of retiring soon? Your dad has to be close to sixty." The questions were really inconsequential.

As Skye waited for his answer, she glanced across the restaurant. The town's retired police chief, Mac Macarthur, sat at the bar talking with Doc Clemson. Some fishermen gabbed with each other across the room. A family with young kids occupied the booth behind them.

Skye's attention returned to the conversation with Ian.

"Retiring? Do you remember my dad?" Ian raised his eyebrows comically. "He loves work more than anything else in life. He'd go crazy if he retired."

"That's great that he found something he loves."

Atticus Winthrop had started a health and beauty care company that mass-produced lotions and shampoos. *Winthrop Cosmetics, a name you can trust.* That was their tagline. And they did everything they could to maintain a wholesome family image.

"It is great. I'm really happy for my dad."

"And how about you? What are you doing? Working for the company?" Ian had always been more of a trust-fund boy who lived off his parents' wealth. But he was twenty-seven now. Certainly he'd grown up some . . . right?

"My dad is training me to take over for him one day. I'm the vice president of sales and marketing right now."

"Impressive."

Ian put his drink down, pressed his arms into the

table, and leaned toward her. "So, let's talk about something more interesting. Who was that guy with you at the beach earlier today? Your boyfriend?"

Skye startled at his directness. "Austin? No. He's just a friend."

Her throat burned as she said the words. She felt like she was lying to herself—especially since she dreamed about what it would be like to date Austin. She only wished that was a possibility.

"You sure? He got that defensive look when I came close, like a dog protecting his territory."

"I think you were reading too much into things." Although Austin's protectiveness was one more reason Skye appreciated him. Being single and without any family in the area, it was nice to have someone to watch her back.

Besides, Austin would never think of her as territory.

Ian smiled—that same satisfied look that he always seemed to wear. "Man, have I mentioned how good it is to see you? You left without a goodbye, Skye."

Skye wanted to tell Ian the truth. To tell him that his parents had paid her to get out of their lives forever. But what good would it do to bring that up now?

"After the baby . . ." Her voice caught as she tried to finish but couldn't.

Ian's smile disappeared, and he reached across the table to squeeze her hand. "I know it was hard for you."

"It was all too painful." That was the truth. When they'd taken her baby from her, it had been gut-wrenching and heartbreaking. Skye had known right away it was a mistake—an irreversible mistake.

"I often wish my parents had never pressed us into giving our baby up." Was that sincerity in Ian's voice? Skye found it hard to believe.

"Me too." Her voice squeaked out.

Not a day went past that she didn't wonder about that child. About what he was like. About how life would have been different if she hadn't signed away her rights.

Skye wanted to ask Ian if his nephew was their son. But the words sounded too crazy, even in her mind. How would they sound when spoken aloud? She opened her mouth, halfway willing to take the risk.

But nothing came out. Her vocal cords seemed to freeze.

"My parents said you went to prison. Is that true?" The question hung suspended in the air as Ian waited for her response.

Skye's heart beat harder in her ears. She glanced around, trying to make sure no one had heard him. This part of her life wasn't something she talked about. No,

Skye didn't want her friends here to know just how much she'd messed up.

She wanted to believe they would accept her with all her ugly flaws and past sorrows. But something else inside her nagged at her and told her they wouldn't. Maybe they'd say nothing had changed, but in their minds, it would have.

The truth was, Skye couldn't accept what she'd done. Why would anyone else?

"Yes, but I shouldn't have been locked up." She raised her chin. "It was all a mistake. I didn't do what I was accused of doing."

No one had believed her then. And she didn't expect Ian to believe her now. But her words were true. And all the money his family had given her? A large portion of it had gone to legal fees. The little bit she'd had left over had been used to move here, buy her produce stand, and start her new life.

"What happened?" He leaned closer, not bothering to hide his curiosity.

"I don't really want to talk about it." Skye tried to forget about that part of her life. She'd erase it totally if she could.

Ian raised a hand and leaned back. "Okay, okay. I get that. It's a sore subject, and I shouldn't have asked. That makes you a little hard-core, though. Which is totally hot."

"There's nothing hot about going to prison."

His raised hand lifted higher. "I get it. Sorry. But it's always been that wild streak that I found so attractive."

"Well, I'm not that person anymore." No, thank goodness, Skye had turned her life around. But she still had a long way to go.

Ian's gaze pierced hers. "Yes, you are. I can see it in your eyes. Once a rebel, always a rebel."

"Could I say the same about you? Once a rich frat boy always a rich frat boy?" She couldn't resist the quip, but she was careful to keep her tone even.

He let out a sharp chuckle. "Ouch. Okay, I see how you are. Maybe people do change."

"You're saying you're different?" Skye had a hard time believing it. Ian still had his swagger, his smug smile, and his expensive toys.

"Yeah, I'm saying I'm different. I'm not the person I used to be." He twisted his head. "You don't look like you believe me."

"I'd like to think we'd both changed, Ian." But on her best days, she doubted herself. And she held almost no hope for Ian.

"So, her old boyfriend is back in town?"

Austin's friend Ty Chambers twisted the top off another water bottle and propped his feet up on the railing of his deck as he waited for Austin to respond.

Austin, Ty, and their friend Wes O'Neill had all gone to Ty's place this evening while his wife, Cassidy, was working. Lately, the new pastor in town—Jack Summers—had been hanging out with them also, but tonight he apparently had other plans.

Ty had thrown on some steaks and fixed some baked potatoes and a salad. They'd eaten until they were full, and now they sat on the screened-in porch, shooting the breeze.

Waves from the ocean rumbled in the background, but darkness masked the shoreline. The strong scent of sea air still lingered around them, mingling with the aroma of their leftover food.

Skye always said the salty air was a cure for everything. Austin wasn't sure about that, but he'd always liked hearing her take on life. She was unlike anyone he'd ever met before—and that was a good thing.

Austin took a long sip of his sweet tea—also compliments of Ty—and remembered his friend's question. "That's right. This guy showed up there on the beach, looking like your typical spoiled rich kid . . . only he's not a kid."

"How did Skye react?" Wes asked.

"Skye was . . . surprised." Austin replayed her reaction in his head. "They're having dinner together now."

"You should tell her how you feel," Ty said. "Why are you waiting? You've liked her since you met her. You even tried to get her out of your head by dating those other women. It didn't work."

Austin leaned back into the weathered Adirondack chair and set his glass on his knee. "I'm waiting because Skye keeps remaining at a distance. I can read the signs. She's not ready."

"Maybe she just needs to know for sure," Wes said. "Women like to be reassured."

Wes was a fine one to talk about women. Austin had heard the town scuttlebutt. The single ladies around Lantern Beach liked to fake plumbing problems just so Wes would come over to help them. He seemed clueless about it all, but the sparkle in his eyes told a totally different story.

Austin supposed that here on Lantern Beach everyone had their secrets, though.

Even Austin.

"If I tell Skye how I feel and she doesn't feel the same way, our friendship will be ruined." That was the bottom-line.

"Not necessarily," Ty said.

"But it could," Wes agreed.

"I guess you have to decide what you want," Ty said. "Some of the best things in life require taking a risk. Is Skye a risk worth taking?"

"Of course she is. I'd do anything for her." Austin thanked God every day that he'd met her when she'd hired him to build the pergola. He'd even taken a loss on the project when he'd realized Skye didn't have the money to pay what he'd normally charge.

He'd found every excuse to go back to her produce stand after that. Finally, he'd invited Skye to Bible study. Their friendship had grown from there.

"I can see the hurt in her eyes," Ty said. "I know she's carrying some burdens, probably from her past. We all do."

"Yes, we all do." Austin had his own set of problems and hurts. He was trying to find resolution, though. Thus his secret project was underway.

But the more Austin thought about this conversation, the more he thought about Skye having dinner with Ian, it made him realize that maybe he should just lay everything out there and stop holding back. Skye was a grown woman. She could make her own choices. If she didn't want to be with him, she'd tell him. Then they could both move on.

Although Austin couldn't stand the thought of not having her in his life.

Just then, his phone buzzed. He looked at the screen and grunted.

"What is it?" Wes asked.

"I'm testing out this new security system for one of my clients," Austin said. "It alerts you whenever a door or window in the house is opened."

"And?" Ty said.

"I installed it at my place to see how it worked. I just got a notice that my door opened."

Ty peered at his phone screen. "Is there a camera also?"

"There is. But when I click on the link, everything is black." Austin squinted. "Strange. I guess I should head over and check things out, just in case."

"Call us if you need us," Wes said.

Austin hoped that wouldn't be necessary.

CHAPTER FIVE

SKYE STARED at the computer screen, just as she'd been doing for hours.

First, last night after she'd gotten home from her dinner with Ian. And now, this morning, after a sleepless night.

Thankfully, her niece Serena was out of town—she was a bridesmaid in a wedding down in Florida. The inquisitive college student asked too many questions— questions Skye wasn't ready to answer. Not yet. No, Skye wasn't ready to share any of this.

Because the ideas seemed too absurd in her mind.

She leaned back and mentally reviewed the facts she'd learned.

Ian's sister Emma Winthrop Harrington had a baby eight years ago.

That was approximately the same time Skye had given her baby up for adoption.

Emma and her husband only had one child. They'd named him *Briar*.

And in every picture Skye had seen of them online, they looked like a happy, all-American family.

There was only one problem. Briar looked just like Skye.

She leaned back into her chair and rubbed her forehead, feeling a headache coming on. Why hadn't Skye heard about this before now? She would have jumped to the same conclusions all those years ago that she did today.

But the news had somehow been concealed from her.

Skye knew the truth about why.

It was because she'd been in prison. She hadn't watched the news while she was there. No, she'd read and drawn pictures and tried to survive.

When Skye had been released, she'd wanted to start a new life, away from her old life and bad influences. Her older sister—the one family member she kept in touch with—had moved up to Michigan.

So Skye had moved here to Lantern Beach. She'd changed her last name. She'd tried to forget about the Winthrops.

And it hadn't been hard. The only time she ever heard

the news was when her friend Wes insisted on sharing that week's top stories. Otherwise, she didn't really care about the stock market, or politics, or what the latest fashion trends were.

All of that might have worked to her detriment, though.

Had Skye been blind all these years to the fact that the Winthrop family may have kept her baby? Had they paid her off so she'd leave, hoping she wouldn't ever learn the truth?

It seemed unbelievable.

And gut-wrenching.

But like a real possibility.

Skye had to figure out how to handle this.

She glanced at her watch, realizing she'd become absorbed in her quest for information. It was nearly ten o'clock.

Skye had to get to work.

But first, she just wanted to search one more thing.

She typed in Ian's name, and pages of results came up. The man definitely had a social media presence. And it was just as Skye had thought.

Her ex hadn't changed.

As recently as three weeks ago, Ian had pictures of himself on his yacht with three different women. He was at popular night clubs and partying in Tel Aviv. Money was no problem for him.

But for someone trying to establish himself and take over his father's company, he sure wasn't showing much maturity.

Skye sighed and stood, her headache pounding hard now. She needed time to sort all of this out. But right now she would go to work. She only hoped she sold enough today to pay her bills because money was getting tight. Too tight for her comfort.

Austin ran a hand through his hair as he rode down the street in his truck, headed for another day of work.

He'd gotten back to his place last night, and everything had checked out fine, despite the notification from his security system. There was no sign anyone had been in his house, and most likely the security equipment had just malfunctioned.

Yet, despite that, he hadn't been able to sleep last night. No, he'd been too busy thinking about Skye. About her old boyfriend who'd rolled into town. Wondering how their dinner had gone. Wondering if Ian was her type.

They were stupid questions. Yet he couldn't deny the tension he felt tugging furiously inside him.

He pulled over to the side of the road, into a gravel lot near Skye's produce stand. He hopped out and sauntered over toward the baskets filled with kale, spinach, apples, and onions.

Skye stepped from the shaded area under the wooden shelter, and a smile lit her face when she saw him.

Just like it did every day.

It was the main reason he stopped here.

"Hey, Austin," she called. "I was wondering if you'd forgotten about me this morning."

As Skye stepped closer, Austin saw that she was using the bottom of her tank top to transport some apples to one of the baskets.

"I could never forget about you, Skye."

Her cheeks reddened. "I almost think you mean it."

I do. He kept the words silent. Instead he asked, "How was your dinner last night?"

The question wouldn't leave his mind.

She shrugged and began to place the apples. "Nothing too exciting. We just caught up with each other. There are a lot of years between us."

"I never took you as the type to run with the rich crowd." *That was subtle, Austin.*

"I'm not that type." She picked up one of the apples she'd just placed and shined it with the hem of her skirt. "Ian . . . he was another lifetime ago."

"I see." Austin could barely take his eyes off the woman with her soft curves and natural beauty. But he had to before he looked like a creep. "Business busy today?"

She let out a little snort. "No. Not at all. I mean, I remember from last year that things slow way, way down during the off-season. I thought I'd prepared for it, but maybe I haven't."

"What do you mean?"

Skye shrugged again and straightened some bundles of kale leaves. "I mean, it's really hard to make a living here on the island. This produce stand isn't a year-round business, and I'm not sure if I make enough money in just the summer to sustain myself. You're not looking for any extra help on the construction site, are you?"

Austin let out a chuckle, trying to picture Skye being content in his line of work. But, now that she brought it up, there was something he'd been thinking about. "I don't really need help on the construction side of things, but I have been playing with an idea lately."

Skye raised her chin in curiosity. "What's that?"

"I'll take you and show you sometime."

"Oh, now you're keeping me in suspense."

He grinned. "I know."

"That's mean."

He wanted to tell her his idea. But the timing needed

to be right. Because what he had in mind could only be temporary . . . but what he really wanted was a future with Skye—a future that included her by his side doing the things they loved.

Now he just needed to think of a way to convince her of the same.

"Well, don't keep me in suspense too long." Skye raised an eyebrow playfully.

"How about tonight?" Austin couldn't pass up the opening.

Skye was silent a moment before nodding. "Okay, tonight."

Pleasure stretched through him. Tonight. Maybe tonight would be a changing point in their relationship. Maybe this was the right time to risk everything.

He picked up an apple, tossed it in the air, and pulled out some money to pay for it. His hand brushed Skye's as he placed the change in her outstretched palm.

Something close to electricity zipped through him. Did Skye feel it too?

Based on the way Skye's cheeks reddened, she had.

She cleared her throat, absently beginning to polish some apples with her skirt again. "By the way, the new haircut makes you look awfully respectable."

Austin raked his hand through his hair again. He'd just gotten his ponytail cut off two weeks ago. It was becoming too high-maintenance. "I thought it was time for a change."

Skye smiled, almost shyly. "I like it. And I can't wait to hear about this idea of yours."

"Tonight, then.

"I'll see you then."

And Austin would count down the minutes until it was time.

CHAPTER SIX

BEFORE LUNCHTIME, Skye put out her donation box at the produce stand. She was trying a new honor system on slow days. And today was a slow day. Besides Austin, she'd only had two other customers. That equaled four hours of work for ten dollars in profit.

The facts were disheartening.

Since Lisa had decided to close the Crazy Chefette on Tuesdays and Wednesdays in the off-season, the two of them were going to meet at a local picnic area on the sound. Lisa was bringing lunch with her.

It would be good to catch up with her friend. But Skye couldn't tell her friend the whole truth about everything going on in her life right now. No way.

Skye pedaled up to the park, left her bike on the sidewalk, and found Lisa at a picnic table facing the water, a basket beside her. Skye paused for just a minute to absorb everything around her. The maritime birds sang their songs. The reeds rustled in the wind. Kiteboarders skimmed over the water as their colorful sails decorated the sky.

All in all, the day seemed pretty perfect outside. Not to mention that it was sixty-eight degrees and sunny in October.

"Hey there," Skye called.

Lisa turned and smiled. "It's the perfect day to be outside enjoying this weather. And I brought your favorite —a shrimp salad wrap with fruit salad."

"It sounds perfect. Thank you."

They pulled out the food and began eating, making small talk.

"So, if you don't mind me asking—who was that guy you were with last night?" Lisa asked, eating the last of her wrap.

"An old boyfriend."

Her eyebrows shot up. "He was cute."

"Oh, he's cute alright. And he's trouble."

"Did he come here to see you?"

"No, I don't think he had any idea I was here." Skye frowned as she remembered Briar. How could she not have known about him for all these years? Why hadn't she looked up information on the family earlier? She'd been beating herself up about it all day.

Easy. Because never in a million years would Skye have guessed that they might have gotten rid of her and adopted her son themselves.

Her stomach still clenched at the thought.

"Everything okay?" Lisa asked. "You look like you're thinking deep thoughts."

"That's one way to say it. I think I just need someone to talk to so I can make sure I'm not going crazy."

"Then I'm your girl." Lisa shoved a Tupperware container toward her. "Have a bacon and chocolate chip cookie and talk to me."

Skye stared at the cookies a moment before finally picking one up. She'd had them before and knew they were surprisingly tasty. But the thought of what they were made of always turned her stomach.

She picked at the cookie, unable to eat it, and finally dove into the conversation before she lost her courage. "I think someone has been lying to me for almost a decade."

Lisa's eyes widened, and she frowned. "I'm so sorry. What can I do?"

Skye's gaze flickered up to her friend's. "How would you find out the truth if you were in my shoes?"

Lisa twisted her lips in thought. "Well, can you ask

this person? I realize he or she may not be truthful. But maybe they would be."

"I suppose I could." She imagined how that would play out. Probably not well.

"Then why not start there? Sometimes the easiest solution is the best one. My mom used to always say that."

"Sounds like good advice. Maybe I'll do that." Skye shook her head. "Now that I'm talking to you, the answers seem simple."

"Sometimes it helps just to say things aloud."

Skye nodded. "You're right."

Lisa shifted. "So, does this have something to do with your ex-boyfriend?"

Skye shrugged. "It's . . . messy."

"What does Austin think about all of this?"

She stole a glance at her cookie and put it down. "I'm not sure. Why does it matter?"

Lisa's head fell to the side. "Really?"

"Really what?"

"You've got to know that Austin looks like he won the lottery every time you come close."

"We're just friends. I'm not really sure he likes me in that way."

Lisa planted her elbows on the table and leaned closer. "Skye, please tell me you're not that naïve."

She wasn't naïve, but she and Austin had never really

talked about taking their relationship any further. Sometimes she thought it was because Austin could see through her—that he could see the messes from her past—and he held her at arm's length. She had so much baggage that she wasn't sure anyone in his right mind could handle it all.

"We're just good friends," Skye finally said.

"You want to know a secret? Austin doesn't even like fruits and vegetables."

"That's ridiculous. He comes to my stand every day and buys something—" Skye stopped herself.

"Exactly. He goes there every day and buys something. Not because he's a health food fanatic, but because it's a great excuse to see you."

Skye's cheeks burned. Was her friend telling the truth? Lisa had no reason to lie to her.

And deep inside, maybe Skye knew that Austin liked her. She'd just been trying to deny it.

She had a lot to think about.

"I should go," she finally muttered. "Thanks for listening, Lisa."

"Any time, Skye."

As Skye walked back out to her bike, she paused. The hair on her arms rose. She turned around. Absorbed the sight of two cars in the lot. One car driving past.

Maybe she was losing her mind.

Because she almost felt like someone was watching her.

But that was impossible since no one else was around.

Austin was going to open up to Skye. He'd thought about it all night and had prayed over his friends' advice. And now it was time to stop wondering and pondering and to take action.

He carefully paced to the other side of the scaffolding so he could continue to replace the damaged shingles on a rental house. The place was located on the sound and stood a massive four stories high with multiple decks, alcoves, and a gable roof and dormers.

Unfortunately, Austin was on the fourth story. He'd purposefully waited for a day when the wind wasn't as strong as it had been, just for safety reasons. It definitely wasn't a job for someone who was afraid of heights.

He glanced down and saw marsh grasses on one side and sand on the other. This was the downside to these houses. Most of them were up on stilts to begin with, making them even more towering.

Now that the busiest part of tourist season was over, a lot of homeowners had started to fix problems that had accumulated over the summer season. That meant that

Austin had a nice roster of jobs lined up for the next couple of months.

The nice part about life here on Lantern Beach was that he could take whatever odd jobs he wanted when he wanted. It was quite the change from his days as an engineer back in Pennsylvania. He'd thought that was the life he wanted, but sitting in an office all day had made him feel as if his life was empty, and the future looked even bleaker. He'd given up the stability of steady work and a nice paycheck to follow his dreams instead.

He hammered another cedar shingle into the side of the house, making sure everything was in place. He wanted to build a reputation around the island as someone people could trust. So far, he had a great stable of clients. He wanted that to continue.

Austin wanted to make a life here. He wanted to grow old on these shores. He wanted to have children and for their toes to be sandy and their hair salty as they learned to chase seagulls and hunt ghost crabs. Life here, in his opinion, was so much better than life anywhere else.

Other than a few random crimes, this place was wholesome and safe.

He was so glad he'd given up everything to come here.

Now he just needed to convince Skye that her dreams and his dreams aligned.

He walked to the other side of the scaffolding, ready to replace more shingles when he felt something shift.

Austin froze and looked down.

One of the legs on his scaffolding wobbled.

He glanced around, looking for a way to stop the inevitable.

But before he could brace himself, the footing beneath him gave away. Air surrounded him as he fell toward the ground.

CHAPTER SEVEN

SKYE RANG the doorbell at the bright blue house located on Ritzy Row. Her throat felt like sandpaper. Like someone had poured scalding hot water down it. Right after she swallowed scissors.

She couldn't do this. What had she been thinking?

Directly asking the Winthrop family if they'd lied to her was the worst idea ever.

She turned around, ready to flee. It wasn't too late to stop before she dug herself into a hole.

But before she even reached the second step, the door opened and a small voice said, "Can I help you?"

Skye's lungs filled with cement. She didn't have to turn around to know who'd answered.

But she turned around anyway. Briar stood there wearing jeans and a surfing T-shirt.

Her heart pounded so hard she feared it might tear through her chest.

"Can I help you, ma'am?" the boy asked again, staring at her with a wide, innocent gaze.

Moisture filled Skye's eyes as she soaked in his face. The broad space between his eyebrows. The inquisitive gaze. The high cheekbones. Just like Skye—only with Ian's startling blue eyes.

"Hi," she finally said, licking her lips as her voice came out as a squeak. "How are you?"

He nodded, ever polite. "I'm fine. And you?"

"Oh, I'm just fine also. Thank you. You're quite the gentleman, aren't you?"

"My mom has very strict ideas on how I should behave." Was that sadness in his voice when he said the words?

Skye wasn't sure. Maybe she imagined it. Maybe she wished it upon him. Wished he was unhappy and uncared for so Skye could snatch him back into her life with good reason.

She cringed. On second thought, maybe "snatched" was the wrong word . . .

"I see," Skye finally said, embarrassed at her thoughts. "Are you feeling okay after your scare yesterday?"

Briar twisted his head—just like Ian always did. "You know about that?"

"I was on the beach when it happened."

He nodded, accepting her answer. "I'm fine. Thank you."

Just then, Ginger Winthrop appeared behind him. Her eyes widened with shock when she spotted Skye standing there. Her hands went to Briar's shoulders, and she pulled him toward her.

Was that casual? Protective?

Maybe Skye was reading too much into this.

"If it isn't Skye." Ginger's voice nearly cracked with tension. "You haven't aged a bit. Still the exotic beauty you always were."

"You haven't aged a bit either." Skye nodded, suddenly mirroring Ginger's stiff politeness.

Ginger's hands continued to grip Briar's shoulders. "What brings you here?"

Skye licked her lips again. "I was hoping to talk to Ian."

"He's not here right now."

"Do you know when he'll return?" Skye glanced at Briar again, her heart aching. Accusations wanted to fly from her lips. But she knew the best way to handle this was to start with Ian. She should have asked him last night at dinner, even if it made her look like a fool.

"He's out sailing with his father. You know how those things go." She offered another stiff smile.

Maybe Skye should ask Ginger the question burning in her mind. Why not? She should just get this over with instead of beating around the bush. But not in front of Briar. She wouldn't put the boy in that position.

Just then, her phone buzzed. Someone was trying to call her.

Skye ignored it. She would check her messages later.

"You're looking well," Ginger continued, her eyes still cold and distant but polite. The woman had perfected the mix.

"Island life agrees with me."

"Yes, it does. I never imagined we'd run into you here."

Ginger probably thought Skye would end up in a drug rehab somewhere. Or six feet under after an overdose. Or . . . well, anywhere but living a halfway normal—and decent—life.

Skye's phone rang again. Who was trying to call her?

"We have a lazy river in our backyard," Briar announced, oblivious to the tension in the air.

Skye forgot about the phone call and bent down to talk with the boy. "Is that right?"

"You should come over and try it out. It's so much fun."

"That sounds like it could be fun. I've always wanted to try out a lazy river."

"It's the coolest thing." His voice climbed with excitement. "I want to get one in my backyard, but my mom said no."

"Well, at least you can come here and use this one." Skye smiled, already feeling a connection with the boy.

Her phone buzzed with two short vibrations in a row letting her know she had a text message.

She straightened and frowned. "Would you two excuse me for one minute?"

One phone call she could ignore. Two? That was pushing it. But a follow-up text? It sealed the deal.

She looked down at her screen and saw a message from Ty.

Call me. It's urgent. About Austin.

If Ty was telling her something was urgent, then it must be. Skye's heart raced.

"I've got to go," Skye rushed. "I'm sorry, but something important came up. Could you tell Ian I stopped by."

"Of course."

Skye paused before turning away. "And it was great talking to you, Briar."

"You too. Come back for the lazy river some time."

Oh, wouldn't the Winthrops love that?

Skye's phone was already to her ear, returning Ty's

phone call as she reached the sidewalk. He answered on the first ring.

"Skye, thanks for calling. There's been an accident . . ."

~

Skye's heart pounded out of control as she rushed between vehicles on her bike. Why couldn't she have brought her car today of all days?

But she hadn't.

Instead, she pushed her muscles as hard as they would go. All she could think about was Austin.

Ty said he was okay, but Skye had been around enough of these kinds of things to know better. What might start as a fall could turn into a blood clot or hemorrhaging later.

She pictured Austin when he'd stopped by the produce stand earlier, just like he did every day. It was one of her favorite parts of the day.

He'd bought an apple.

Were Lisa's words correct? Did Austin not even like fruits or vegetables? Could it be true that he just stopped by to see her, at the most, or to support her business, at the least?

She didn't know. All she knew was that her life

wouldn't be nearly as bright without him. Actually, bright was an understatement. She'd come to rely on Austin in ways she shouldn't. He was one of her best friends, and she couldn't imagine the future without him.

She might even love him.

She sucked in a breath at the thought. No, the idea was crazy. And now wasn't the time to deal with it. First she had to figure out Briar.

Finally, she reached Austin's bungalow—a small cottage with a loft that served as a bedroom and a large wooded lot surrounding it. She hopped off her bike and darted toward the front door, anxious to see Austin for herself.

Before she reached the door, Cassidy stepped outside and stopped her.

"Is he okay? What happened?" The questions rushed from Skye as she tried to read the expression on Cassidy's face.

Cassidy gripped her arm, her voice calm and reassuring. "Austin's going to be fine. It could have been much worse. He just has a few scrapes and bruises."

"What happened?" Skye willed her heart to slow, but it wouldn't. Not until she saw Austin for herself.

"He was working four stories up when his scaffolding malfunctioned," Cassidy said. "He fell, but, thankfully, landed in the marsh. If he hadn't . . . well, it would be a different story right now. Someone was watching out for him."

Thank God he'd landed in the marsh. Cassidy was right. He might not have survived otherwise.

"I want to see him," Skye said.

Cassidy released Skye's arm. "Of course. He's inside. And he's being stubborn. See if you can get him to take some pain meds and lie low for the rest of the day. Neither Ty nor I had any luck."

Skye nodded, even though she barely heard the words. She skirted past Cassidy and through the front door. Finally, her gaze fell on Austin. He really was alive and okay.

Austin stood from the couch, his motions stiff as he rose to greet her. Skye stepped close, something fierce and strong gripping her heart. Concern? Worry? Love?

She stopped just short of being in Austin's arms and studied him, making sure she'd understood Cassidy correctly. His bicep was wrapped in gauze. A cut was together by butterfly bandages on his forehead. Another cut sliced across his neck.

Skye reached forward and started to touch it but stopped herself.

Suddenly, she was all too aware of how close she'd stepped to Austin. Of how easy it would be to reach up and touch him. To kiss him. To show him all the emotions she felt inside. To let him know how much she cared.

But those desires were quickly met by memories from her past.

"You gave me a good scare." Her voice trembled as she stared up at him.

"I had a good scare myself." He stared back at her, a strange yet compelling look in his eyes. A look that connected them, that somehow drew them together.

"I'm so glad you're okay, Austin," she practically whispered. She wasn't sure where all the feelings were coming from or why they were rushing to the surface right now. She only knew that she never wanted to lose this man. Never.

CHAPTER EIGHT

SKYE REACHED her arms around Austin and pulled him into a hug. As his arms circled around her, his touch sent shivers up her spine.

She rested her head on his chest, relishing the feel of his heart pounding against her face. She took a deep breath, inhaling the scent of sweat and sawdust and minty aftershave. The combination was fantastic.

But she had to get a grip. She couldn't let her emotions supersede logic.

She stepped back and cleared her throat. "What happened exactly?"

Austin's face fell with . . . disappointment? Or was she reading too much into things?

Whatever had gone wrong was a big deal. This wasn't

the Austin she knew. The Austin Skye knew was strong and nearly invincible. This accident had taken a toll on him.

"I was over at the Seagull Palace replacing some shingles. I've been working on it for the past few days."

"That's that huge house, right?" She glanced behind him at the couch, realizing Austin needed to sit down. Taking his arm, Skye led him to the sofa and gently shoved him until he got comfortable on the cushions.

"Bossy much?"

"Only when it comes to important stuff. Now, continue." She sat beside him and grabbed his hand.

"Yes, Seagull Palace is tall. Really tall. Four stories and on stilts. Anyway, my scaffolding was set up, just like it always is. I checked it before I climbed up. I don't know what happened, but one of the legs collapsed, and the whole thing went down."

Skye closed her eyes as she pictured it playing out. "Where were you when it happened?"

"On the top."

She squeezed his hand harder as the implications of his statement washed over her. "You could have died."

Austin didn't deny her words. "You're right. I could have. But, by the grace of God, I didn't. I only have a few cuts and bruises. I'll be sore tomorrow, for sure."

"Doc Clemson checked you out?"

"He did. He said I'm fine."

Austin wiped her cheeks with the back of his fingers again.

Skye hadn't even realized she'd started crying.

Austin released a soft, teasing chuckle. "If I'd known getting hurt would make me feel so special, I would have gotten injured a long time ago."

Skye swatted his chest, thankful that he was trying to lighten the moment. "Stop it. I had worst-case scenarios going through my mind."

His smile slipped. "I didn't mean to worry you."

She wiped the rest of the moisture from her cheeks, straightened, and drew in a deep breath, as if she were pulling herself together. "I guess you're not going to be able to show me your surprise tonight."

"Says who?"

"Everyone would say that. You need to rest after your accident."

"Don't be ridiculous. I'm fine." He reached to the table beside him, grabbed his car keys, and handed them to Skye. "Besides, you could drive, if that would make you feel better."

She raised her eyebrows. "You'd trust me with your truck?"

He loved his truck and wasn't the type to let other people drive it.

"Of course I would," he said.

She remained quiet a moment before finally nodding slowly. "Okay, then. Where are we going?"

"I'll tell you when we get there." Pleasure rippled through his voice.

"You're a tease. Have I ever told you that before?"

"More than once." He smiled.

"You're sure you're up for doing this?"

"I'm positive. A little ride in my truck isn't going to hurt anything."

Finally, Skye nodded. "Okay, then. Let's go."

Austin had seen it in Skye's eyes.

She cared for him just as much as he cared about her. She might not admit it. She might not be ready for a relationship. But she cared about him.

That realization brought Austin a surge of delight.

There was no one else he'd rather be with right now. He wanted his future to be with Skye, and he was tired of pretending like he didn't.

He glanced at her as she drove his goliath of a truck down the highway. The darkness of early evening had begun to spread across the sky outside. Skye's hair shone every time they passed a street light. Her pleasant profile looked determined as she stared at the road ahead.

This was what he wanted. Forever. Him and Skye.

"Turn here," he said

She followed his directions and turned down a gravel road. The headlights showed scraggily bushes and trees on either side of the truck as they bumped farther down the road.

Skye didn't seem to mind. She didn't flinch or show any fear or distrust.

The woman was a mystery like that. Sometimes fearful and insecure, and other times brave and fearless. It fascinated him.

"Stop here," he told her.

She pressed the brakes and stared out the front window. A wrinkle of confusion formed between her eyes. "It's a house. Or, a shack, I should say."

Austin smiled and climbed from the truck, ignoring the way his body ached from the fall. There were more important things to concentrate on right now. "Come on."

Skye gave him a skeptical look before climbing out and joining him in the beams of the headlights. He took her hand, and she didn't pull away as he led her up the front steps and unlocked the door. He stepped inside and flicked on the lights.

The musty, old cottage came into view.

Skye glanced around, her gaze stretching up to the cathedral ceiling and back down to the ugly carpet. "Wow, I have to say that I have no earthly idea what to think of this surprise."

Austin smiled at the dry tone of her voice. "This is mine."

She turned toward him, her gaze full of questions. "You have a place that's nicer than this."

He nodded, unable to argue, and looked back at the house. "I don't plan on living here. I'm going to fix it up."

"And sell it?"

"Or rent it."

Skye released his hand and took a step forward, her head angled upward as she soaked in all the details. "The place has good bones."

Yes, it did. Three bedrooms. Two stories. Outdated. Neglected. But it had tons of potential.

"That's what I thought too. Sure, it needs to be fixed up. But this could be some place great. A place where families can make memories and relax and breathe as they get away from the stress of their normal lives."

"I agree. It has a lot of possibilities." She stopped her perusing and turned back to him. "This sounds like a great opportunity for you, but I'm not sure what this has to do with me."

Austin wanted to pour out his dreams of marrying

her. Of taking on projects like this together. But that might send Skye running away from here faster than a prisoner who'd just escaped a life sentence. "I want your vision, Skye."

"My vision is looking at you right now like you're crazy."

He chuckled. He couldn't resist grabbing her hand and tugging her closer. "No, you've got a great eye for decorating and design. And you're great at doing things on a budget. You take items that other people have discarded, and you make them beautiful. You create artwork out of shells and sticks. I can do the basics here, Skye, but I want your help in making this place inviting."

Her cheeks flushed. "I would love to do something like that, Austin."

Satisfaction warmed his chest. "I thought you might."

"But how would that work? I mean, practically speaking, what are you thinking?"

That we could get married. He didn't say that. "I have a few projects I need to finish up, and then I want to spend the winter months working here. I thought we could negotiate a flat fee for your services."

"I have no training," she reminded him. "Just gut instinct."

"That's worth a lot. We could talk about a price that's

fair. You could help me, and it would be a win-win for both of us."

Austin stared at Skye, watching for her reaction. She looked contemplative but finally a grin stretched across her face.

"I love that idea, Austin."

His expression mirrored hers. "I was hoping you'd say that."

As natural as if they'd done it a million times before, Skye flung her arms around his neck in an embrace. They held each other for a few minutes in silence, Austin ignoring his aches and pains and cuts and bruises. He wouldn't let them ruin this moment.

"What's this for?" he asked.

"For being you. For this opportunity. For everything." Gratitude etched her voice.

Austin pressed his head into the top of hers, the words on the tip of his tongue. Words about how much he cared for her and wanted to be more than friends.

Before any of them could leave his lips, Skye raised her head, and their gazes caught.

Something deep passed between them, connecting them.

Austin's hand cupped her face. His other hand moved from around her waist to her hair and tangled in the locks there. His gaze went to her lips.

But before their lips connected, a noise jerked them from the moment. The sound snapped them back to reality so quickly that Austin felt like he'd touched fire.

Skye backed away, shaking her head. "I'm sorry. Excuse me a minute."

She reached into her purse and pulled out her phone. Her hands visibly trembled as she put the device to her ear. "Hello?"

Her face went pale as she murmured a few indecipherable things to the person on the other line. Finally, she hit End and turned back to him.

"I'm sorry, Austin, but I've got to run."

His heart panged with disappointment. "Right now?"

Skye nodded, her gaze still apologetic. She touched his arm a moment before slipping her hand back to her side and staring at his chest. "I'm sorry. I really am. But this can't wait."

"Is there something I can help you with?"

"No, I have to do this alone."

His chest throbbed. Why wouldn't she let him inside her life? What kinds of secrets did she hide in the depths of her luminous brown eyes?

Even more—would she ever trust him enough to share?

Finally, Austin stepped back and nodded. "Okay,

then. It's a good thing your bike is in the back of the truck. I'll drop you off. Just name the place."

She seemed to drag her gaze back up to his as she nodded and mumbled, "Thank you."

Maybe it was better this way—better if they took more time to talk before they dove into something where they both might get hurt.

CHAPTER NINE

SKYE'S HEART rate continued to accelerate as Austin drove her toward the beach.

How would Ian react to this conversation? She had no idea.

But she had to ask these questions—no matter what the outcome was.

As Austin pulled to a stop, she stared out the window and shivered. The next thing she knew, Austin had taken off his flannel shirt and handed it to her. "Here, take this. You're going to get chilly."

She took the soft piece of clothing from him, gratitude filling her. "Thank you, Austin."

"I'll wait here for you."

"I can just take my bike—"

"I'd feel better if I waited."

Finally, she nodded. "Okay, then. Thank you."

With one last glance at Austin, she climbed out.

She hated to do this right now, especially after everything that had happened. First, Austin's accident. Then his revelation about wanting her help to fix up that house.

She wanted to revel in the possibilities of working with Austin.

If she were honest with herself, she'd admit that what she really wanted, even more than that, was to indulge in thoughts about their almost kiss.

She hadn't imagined that, had she? No, she hadn't. If her phone hadn't rung . . .

But this wasn't the time for it. Right now, she had other pressing matters.

She made her way toward one of the wooden community swings beneath a pergola that faced the ocean. A few people were out right now, even though it was dark outside.

But there was only one person she focused on—the lone figure on the swing.

Ian.

She'd recognize him anywhere.

Her palms felt sweaty as she lowered herself beside him. But Ian didn't appear nervous at all. A bright smile lit his face. Then again, he was the kind of person who thrived on conflict—it was just one more reason they were so bad together.

"Hey, beautiful." He patted the space beside him.

Skye didn't scoot closer, though. "Thanks for coming."

"I couldn't pass up spending more time with you."

And there he went, being charming and charismatic—all the things that had originally drawn Skye to him. She'd been so lost and alone. He'd been secure and had offered companionship—or, should she say, trouble?

She should have been pickier, though. Why was hindsight always twenty-twenty?

"So, what's going on, Skye High?"

She'd always hated that nickname. She licked her lips and decided to ignore him and get right to the point. "Do you ever think about our son?"

Ian's gaze darkened. "Of course I do. Why are you asking?"

"I think about him all the time. I wonder how he's doing. What he looks like. If he ended up with a good family."

"I'm sure he's doing fine. I know it's probably hard for you, not knowing."

Skye shifted to face him, willing her voice not to quiver. "It's more than hard. I've regretted my choice every day."

"I'm sure that's normal. There's always some regret involved with things like this. It was a big decision."

"It's not normal regret. It's not regret because I know I made the right choice, even though it was hard. It's regret because I felt pressured into doing something I didn't want to do."

"What are you saying, Skye?" Ian narrowed his eyes and studied her face.

"Your parents kept telling me how I wasn't in a good place to raise a baby," she reminded him.

"You weren't. Neither was I."

"Your mom told me I wouldn't be a good mom, and that I was too messed up. That the baby would be better off without me."

Ian grabbed her hand. "I'm sorry, Skye. I didn't know."

"She told me you'd be better off without me. That I created chaos." Skye's voice cracked, but she couldn't stop now. She had to see this through.

"Don't listen to her. She's my mom, and I love her. But she's always been a self-righteous snob."

Skye stared off at the dark horizon, knowing the ocean was there, even though she couldn't see it. "Unfortunately, I began to believe her lies. I convinced myself that I couldn't raise a child and that the baby would be better without me. The thing is, that's not what I thought. Not until your mom convinced me of it."

"I don't know what else to say. I'm sorry, Skye."

She pulled the flannel shirt Austin had let her borrow closer around her neck as tumultuous thoughts rumbled inside her. Finally, she turned back to Ian. Before she chickened out, she blurted, "Is Briar our son, Ian?"

Ian's eyes widened, and then he laughed—a dismissive, surprised laugh. "What? Briar? Skye . . . I'm sorry. No. Why would you ask that?"

Her cheeks heated. "He looks like me. And he looks like you."

"Maybe there are similarities, but that doesn't mean anything, Skye. You're just seeing what you want to see. He looks just like my sister. She and I have the same eyes. She has dark hair like you."

Was Ian right? Was Skye going crazy and letting her mind play tricks on her? "He's the right age."

"You knew my sister and her husband wanted a baby. That was no secret. They were going through IVF."

"And did it work?" Skye watched his face for any sign of deceit.

Ian's expression remained unchanged. "It did. Briar was born about six months after we broke up."

Skye's shoulders sagged. Maybe she had blown all of

this out of proportion. Maybe she'd seen what she wanted to see. Was that it?

"Hey . . ." Ian caught a lock of Skye's hair and brushed it out of her face. "I know this is all a lot. But you just have to put the past behind you. What's done is done."

She nodded, knowing his words were true.

When she realized that his hand rested tangled in her hair, she stood. She couldn't do this. Couldn't go there again.

"I should run," she muttered. "It's getting late."

Ian grabbed her hand as she took a step away. "Skye . . . you probably shouldn't push this." His voice held an edge of warning.

"Push what?"

"Briar. You should let it go."

She jerked her hand away, feeling betrayed. "What are you saying?"

Ian pressed his lips together. "I'm just saying that my parents are a little prickly right now. Bringing this up will only irritate them."

Skye let his words settle, but only for a second before a fire lit in her. "Are you threatening me, Ian?"

He shook his head. "Not at all. I just don't want to see you get hurt."

He didn't want to see her get hurt? Where was that knight in shining armor eight years ago when his parents paid her to leave? Had he fought for her then? No, he hadn't.

"If Briar is Emma's child, then I don't know why anyone would get hurt," Skye finally said.

Ian remained quiet. And that was all the answer Skye needed.

Tears burned Skye's eyes as she climbed into Austin's truck. She wished she'd told him she'd just ride her bike home so she could burn off some emotional energy—she had plenty to burn. It felt like flares erupted inside her.

Memories of that final conversation with Ginger replayed in her mind. *You're not cut out to be a mom. The baby will be better off without you. Some people just shouldn't become parents.*

Earlier she'd wondered if she and Austin had a chance together. But lies mixed with truth inside her until it felt impossible to decipher one from the other.

"Skye?" Austin said.

"I'm sorry." She waved a hand in front of her face. "I don't want to be rude, but I don't want to talk right now. I just need to process."

"That's okay. You don't have to say anything you don't want to say."

Skye was grateful that Austin understood. She pulled her seatbelt on and crossed her arms as she stared out the window.

The questions kept tumbling inside her until she almost felt sick to her stomach.

Ian hadn't answered her inquiry sufficiently. And she couldn't let this go. Ian could be lying. She had to know if Briar really was her son.

But Skye would need to think about how to proceed. She'd need to think about it very carefully.

Skye would also need to think about whatever had almost transpired between her and Austin at the house.

A sense of excitement filled her when she thought about the property he'd bought. At the thought of working as a team to fix it up. It was the first time Skye had become excited at the prospect of her future in a long time. She and Austin . . . they would make a good team.

And maybe more.

But Skye had to let Austin know what he was getting into before they took any kind of plunge together. If Austin was smart, he'd run away. And she would totally understand. She might even applaud him for it.

But she couldn't handle that conversation now. Not until she got her head on straight.

Finally, Austin pulled into the campground where she lived. They passed by a family or group that was obviously partying. They weren't full-timers. Most people around here weren't.

Another trailer had a man sitting outside drinking a beer. He raised it to them as she passed.

Then they reached her RV. Austin climbed out and grabbed her bike, about to stow it next to Elsa, the ice cream truck her niece had purchased from Cassidy. But as he did, he froze.

Austin grabbed Skye and pulled her against his solid chest. He crept backward until they were in the shadows.

What . . .?

As if reading her mind, he nodded toward her RV. She glanced over, desperate to figure out what was going on.

She sucked in a breath when she saw what was out of place.

Was that a light inside her camper?

Not a normal light. No, it appeared to be a beam, like that from a flashlight bouncing in the darkness.

Someone was in her RV.

CHAPTER TEN

AUSTIN STARED at Skye's camper, hoping his eyes were deceiving him.

But, sure enough, there was the beam again.

Someone *was* inside Skye's home.

But why? And who?

Skye drew closer to Austin, her hands clinging to his chest and back and her eyes fixated on the scene.

Austin wouldn't try to be the hero and go inside to confront the intruder. No, he remained in the darkness and waited. Watched.

The light disappeared. A moment later, the door to her camper opened and someone wearing all black stepped out. The person glanced around before slipping behind her RV and out of sight.

"Should we follow him?" Skye whispered.

Austin shook his head. "No, he had a gun."

"What?"

"It was in the holster at his belt. We should call Cassidy."

Carefully, cautiously, they slunk from beside the ice cream truck, trying to remain in the shadows.

Austin desperately wanted a glimpse of who that had been. The dark clothing combined with the darkness outside made it impossible to see any details.

They reached her trailer and slipped toward the corner.

Just as they did, a vehicle roared to life.

Austin peered around the other side just in time to see a dark SUV pull away.

No license plates.

But the bad feeling in Austin's gut grew with every passing moment. He'd been right. Danger was in the air. And it was growing with every passing second.

Skye turned to stare at Austin for a minute after Cassidy left. They stood on the small deck outside her RV, one that stretched across the length of the camper. At the corner, she'd even strung a colorful hammock next to her potted plants. A string of solar powered lanterns helped to define the space and create a cozy atmosphere.

If only Skye felt cozy inside right now. But she felt far from that.

Cassidy hadn't found any evidence of anything stolen or disturbed inside her place.

So why did someone bother to break in?

Skye wasn't sure. But she didn't like this.

"I don't feel right leaving you here alone." Austin stood in front of her, seeming to own the space. Then again, he'd been the one who'd built this deck, so maybe he did.

He was always taking care of her, wasn't he?

"I'll be okay," she insisted. "It's like Cassidy said—nothing was taken or messed up."

"I don't like this, Skye. Someone didn't go into your place for no reason."

She saw the concern in his gaze—and she appreciated it more than he could ever know.

"You need to go home and get your rest. You had a bad fall today, and the last thing you need is to babysit me."

He frowned. "Skye, you know that's not how I look at it."

She gently rested a hand on his chest. "I know. But

you're so busy trying to look after me. Who's going to look after you? Go home. Get some rest. I'll be fine here."

"Okay," Austin said after a moment of quiet. But he still looked unconvinced. "But I need to know you're inside and that your door is locked."

"It's a deal," she murmured.

Skye had the unreasonable urge to reach up and kiss him. She craved feeling his arms around her again—just as she had when he'd pulled her into the shadows. She wanted . . . she wanted more than friendship.

Instead, she stepped back. Her throat ached as she said, "Good night, Austin."

"Good night, Skye."

She forced herself to go inside and lock the door. As she did, she saw Austin finally step away. She changed into some flannel pants and a stretchy T-shirt, but her spirit felt unsettled.

As Skye lowered herself onto her bed, shivers overtook her. Maybe she was overreacting, but she felt violated. This space was hers, and no one else had the right to come inside without her permission.

Why *had* someone broken in? It didn't make sense. She had nothing of value.

And that was the thought that really disturbed her.

Skye pulled her legs into her bed and scooted backward toward her pillow. As she did, she glanced out the window, hoping for a glimpse of moonlight or twinkling stars to comfort her.

Instead, she drew in a quick breath.

Austin was lying in her hammock.

What?

And then Skye realized the truth. He was still protecting her, even if from a distance.

She sucked on her bottom lip a moment. It was entirely too chilly for Austin to sleep out there. Though the days had been unseasonably warm, it was probably only fifty-some degrees out there right now.

Skye stared at him, trying to figure out if she should run him off or . . . do something else. She wasn't sure what.

The moonlight hit him, illuminating his outline. His arms were folded behind his head, as if he were relaxing. She knew that was the last thing Austin was doing, though. No, he was on guard—listening and watching for any more signs of danger.

What had she ever done to deserve someone like Austin in her life?

Before Skye could overthink it, she threw her legs out of bed and grabbed an extra blanket. Quietly, she opened the door to her RV and tiptoed across the deck.

She paused by the hammock and slipped the blanket over him.

Though Austin hadn't moved, his gaze was on her.

"What are you doing?" His voice sounded low and husky.

"I could ask you the same thing. I thought you might need to stay warm."

Skye wasn't sure how it happened. Had Austin extended his arm as an invitation? Had she read too much into things?

Somehow, Skye found herself slipping beside him on the hammock. She rested her head against his chest and pulled the blanket around their shoulders.

Neither said anything.

They didn't need to.

Austin gently kissed the top of her head. When he did, Skye closed her eyes, feeling safe for the first time in forever as she drifted to sleep.

CHAPTER ELEVEN

AUSTIN HADN'T SLEPT all night. No, partly he'd
been awake, listening for signs of danger. The other part
of him had relished the feeling of Skye being in his arms.
They fit together, like two broken pieces had been put
together to form a whole.

He leaned into her, relishing the scent of honeysuckle
and apples. He listened to her steady breathing as she
rested. He felt the soft skin of her arms and hands. He
could picture the two of them doing this . . . forever.

He couldn't deny that he was worried, though. Some
kind of inner turmoil spun inside her. He could see it in
her gaze. And then last night.

Why had someone been in her camper? What wasn't
Skye telling him?

Austin desperately wished that Skye would open up

and share whatever it was that made her gaze so turbulent. But he had to wait for her timing.

Until then, he would hold her. Watch over her. Try to give her the security she needed.

As the sun came up, Skye flinched. Stretched. Yawned.

Finally, her eyes fluttered open.

She tensed and shot up, as if she'd forgotten all her worries for a minute, only to have them come crashing back with a vengeance.

"Morning," he said, a lazy, early morning twang to his voice.

"Morning." Skye touched her mouth and closed her eyes. Was that regret? Austin sure hoped it wasn't. "You . . . you should have gone home last night. You're going to be exhausted today."

"I'll be fine, Skye."

She started to scramble from the hammock, but Austin caught her wrist. "Skye, you're never an inconvenience."

Austin studied her as she processed his words. Skepticism crossed her gaze, then hope.

Then . . . she took his hand into both of hers and closed her eyes.

"Thank you, Austin." Her voice could barely be heard, but the gratitude was evident in her body language.

When she opened her eyes, their gazes caught.

There it was again.

That thing that passed between them. The attraction. The desire. The longing.

He reached up and wiped the hair from her eyes. His hand remained cupping her cheek, and she leaned into his touch.

Maybe a relationship between them wasn't wishful thinking after all.

"Skye, I—"

Before he could finish, a loud voice cut through the air. "Hey, you two!"

Skye jumped to her feet at the intrusion, nearly causing the hammock to flip. Austin jerked a leg onto the deck and stopped himself from toppling to the ground.

When he turned, he saw Jimmy James standing behind them.

Jimmy James was the local town troublemaker, yet somehow the man was still likable. He was a strange mix with his muscular, tattooed arms, and dopey expressions. The guy was nice enough; he just had no moral compass.

"Hey, Jimmy James." Austin sat up, an ache seizing him and reminding him that he could have died yesterday.

"I thought I recognized your truck," Jimmy James continued, oblivious to how awkward his appearance was.

Maybe this was Austin's opportunity to find out some

information. "Hey, did you see anyone over here at Skye's RV last night? Probably around eight o'clock."

Jimmy James grunted and shrugged. "Not really. Why?"

"Just curious."

The man's gaze flickered to Skye. "Someone giving you trouble, Skye? Because I'll keep my eyes open. I like to look out for my friends."

"Thank you, Jimmy James," Skye said. "If you see anyone over here, I'd appreciate it if you'd let me know."

"Of course I will. Us full-timers here at the campground need to stick together."

After he lumbered off, Austin turned to Skye. But before he could speak, she did.

"Listen, I need to get to the produce stand, and then I have a few things to do," she started. "I appreciate you keeping an eye on me last night. It means a lot to me, Austin."

"Maybe you shouldn't be alone today . . ."

"I'll be fine. I'll be safe. I promise. Besides, I know you have work to do as well."

He did have things he needed to get done. But he'd forget about all of it if Skye asked him to. Which she would never do. "I'd feel better if you'd check in with me on occasion, at least."

"I can do that."

Austin nodded, knowing it was the best he was going to get from Skye right now. If he pushed it anymore, she might go running.

And that was the last thing he wanted.

Two hours later, Austin and Wes stared at the four-story house that had almost been the death of Austin yesterday.

"So the scaffolding just collapsed?" Wes asked.

Austin nodded, remembering the moment he'd toppled nearly forty feet from the top and hit the marsh waters. His life had flashed before his eyes, and he hadn't been certain he'd live to see this day. "Apparently."

Wes picked up one of the metal pieces that still lay in the sand and examined it. "That doesn't even sound right. I've worked with you. I know how particular you are about stuff like that, especially when you're working four stories up."

"If there's one thing I've learned, it's to measure twice and cut once. I always double-check these things." Austin trudged through some marsh grass and picked up another piece of the metal that had once been a part of the scaffolding. He squinted as he stared at it, his gut twisting with doubt.

"What is it?" Wes joined him and stared at the piece.

Austin held it out toward him. "Is it just me or does it look like this metal was cut?"

Wes examined the pipe, his eyes narrowing in thought.

"That's a fresh cut. The metal hasn't corroded yet—it's still clean." Wes looked up and met Austin's gaze. "You think someone tampered with it?"

Austin shrugged. "Why would they do that?"

Wes shrugged. "I don't have any great ideas. Didn't a new contractor move into town last month?"

"Jonathan Sanders? He seems like a stand-up guy. I can't imagine he'd do this to sabotage my business. It would be drastic, to say the least."

"Maybe it's a competing homeowner. People are desperate to have their weeks rented out, especially in homes as large as this one."

Austin shook his head, still not buying Wes's ideas. He didn't think Wes did either. "What would that prove? Sure, it would slow down the progress of my work, but it wouldn't scare people away from the house."

"If someone died here it might."

A hollow feeling formed in Austin's gut. Maybe they were offtrack here. But someone had messed with his scaffolding. The only reason they'd do that was to hurt him.

"I'm going to have to tell Cassidy—Chief Chambers, I

should say," Austin said, taking the cut piece of scaffolding from Wes. It was his only evidence.

"She'll always be Cassidy to us, right?"

"Yeah, I guess she will."

Wes's phone buzzed, and his eyes widened when he glanced at the screen.

"Is everything okay?" Austin asked.

Wes nodded—a little too quickly. "Yeah, it's fine."

"Wes . . . ?" There was something he wasn't telling Austin.

His friend released a breath. "I'm sure it's nothing. It was just my friend Colton."

"The one who works with you doing kayak tours?"

"Yeah, he's the one. He was down on the boardwalk last night."

"And?" Austin knew he shouldn't press, but he couldn't help himself. Everyone had so many secrets lately. Including himself.

He needed to end that. Life was short. But he should be able to trust his inner circle with what was going on with him. Maybe Austin had been foolish not to do that in the first place.

Wes cringed and raked a hand across the top of his head. "Colton was asking about the new guy Skye was with."

Austin's spine tightened. "What?"

"He said the two looked like more than friends. They were on a swing down on the boardwalk last night. He said they looked quite friendly."

Austin tried to keep a cool head. He'd known Skye and Ian had met, but he hadn't been able to see them from where he sat parked in his truck. Skye hadn't seemed especially starry eyed afterward.

However, he *had* seen that look in Skye's gaze yesterday. The look that said she liked Austin. That she'd wanted to kiss him. And the woman had definitely been worried about him.

He knew Skye sometimes had that wild, unsettled look in her eyes. But would she really bounce from Austin to someone else that easily?

He didn't think so.

Then why did his insides feel like they were being ripped apart at the thought of Skye being with someone else?

He knew why.

Because he loved her.

CHAPTER TWELVE

SKYE SWUNG by Happy Hippy Produce and set out some new deliveries that had arrived this morning. The fall wasn't always the ideal time for produce stands, but these seasonal fruits and vegetables were some of her favorites.

Greens like kale and collards. Apples. Pumpkins. Gourds.

She loved them all.

She'd also added some hanging flower pots full of mums along with sunflowers and a selection of potted herbs. She was going to have to expand her thinking if she wanted to thrive during the off-season.

She picked up an apple and examined it, just like she did every day. She had to make sure her products were quality. As she continued the inspection, her thoughts wandered to Austin's offer to help him fix up houses.

She liked the idea of making something old and abandoned look beautiful. And she really liked the idea of working with Austin on top of earning some extra money. She wasn't even sure if those additional funds would cut it, though, when it came to paying her bills.

Placing the last apple back into the basket, Skye paused.

She wouldn't stay here at the stand today, she decided. No, she'd put out the good faith donation box and hope she didn't regret the choice.

Other more pressing matters had her attention.

Skye unlocked the donation box to clear out any extra money that had come in before she left.

After grabbing the bills, she was about to lock the box back up when she paused.

Was that a one-hundred-dollar bill?

She narrowed her eyes as she fanned the paper money out.

There were actually *two* hundred-dollar bills inside.

What in the world?

Skye definitely hadn't sold enough produce to justify that amount of money. So who had left it?

Ian, she realized. He was the only one who made sense. Two hundred dollars to him was like two dollars to the average person. Was he trying to pay her off? Or maybe he felt sorry for her?

Skye wasn't sure.

She jammed the money into her purse, vowing to think about it more later on. As she walked to her bike, a truck stopped at the side of the road, and Jimmy James rolled down his window. "Hey, Skye."

"Hey, Jimmy James. You off to work?" The man always seemed fond of her—almost like a big brother. But Skye tried to be careful around him. He represented an old part of her life, a part she didn't want to go back to.

"I'm just leaving," he said. "Business been busy for you?"

She propped her hip against her bike and paused to finish the conversation. "Not really. But I guess that's the way it works around here."

"Yeah, I know what that's like. It can be hard to pay the bills in the winter. At least, it used to be."

Used to be? What did that mean?

Skye thought about all the money she needed to both keep her business going and to pay her bills. "You have some good ways to get some extra cash? Because I need some."

He grinned. "I know a few ways."

Skye shifted her weight to her other hip. "Are they legal ways?"

Jimmy James shrugged, looking like he didn't have a care in the world as he sat there shooting the breeze. "Depends on how you define legal."

"I'm not interested otherwise." Skye couldn't even tempt herself with anything that was less than honorable. That wasn't her life anymore—and it would never be her life again.

"You could make a few deliveries for me. The fees for doing so could really add up, if you're looking for money."

Deliveries? It sounded suspicious. "What kind of deliveries?"

Jimmy James grinned and started pulling away. "What you don't know can't hurt you."

Skye didn't like the sound of that. But the idea of making more money easily was very tempting. She wasn't going to be able to get any extra money from this produce stand—not unless people continued to leave large dollar amounts in her donation box.

But there was no way she'd entertain Jimmy James's offer.

She jumped onto her bike and started down the road.

Today, she was going to keep an eye on the Winthrops. She wanted to know what the family was up to, and it was becoming obvious they would never share on their own. That meant she needed to be creative and find other ways.

Besides, she wanted to see Briar again. Wanted to know he was okay. That he was being taken care of and loved.

She would get answers, and nothing was going to stop her.

Skye parked her bike beneath an empty beach house and climbed the stairs until she reached a screened-in porch.

She knew no one was renting this place right now, and she also knew that the screens would conceal her presence from any onlookers who were out and about today.

This smaller house was right across the street from Ritzy Row, and therefore right across the street from the home the Winthrops were renting.

Maybe this was an act of desperation. Skye knew that. But she didn't care.

Besides she was out of options. If she were rich and wealthy like the Winthrops, she could pay people to do this for her. She could hire a private investigator and a lawyer. She could talk to people in power who could bend the law to meet their demands.

But that wasn't Skye. She had little to no resources.

So she would do what she could.

She settled on a squeaky porch swing and watched

the house across the street, rhythmically letting her seat sway back and forth.

After two hours, she'd seen nothing. Four cars—all luxury vehicles—sat in the driveway unmoving.

The front door hadn't even opened.

For all she knew, the family wasn't here and this was all for nothing.

Skye's thoughts went back to Briar.

How would Skye's life look different if Briar was hers? She had signed away her rights and had no legal means of changing that.

But now that she'd seen the boy . . . now that she knew he could be her son . . . all she wanted was to be a part of his life.

Was the thought crazy? Skye didn't know.

Her phone rang. It was Austin. She'd promised to check in and hadn't done so yet.

"Hey, there," she answered.

"Hey, I hadn't heard from you in a while. Everything okay?"

Delight filled her when she heard his smooth, deep voice. She stared at the house across the street and considered how to respond. "Yeah, everything is fine."

"What are you doing?" he asked.

Skye couldn't very well tell him she'd invaded

someone else's screen porch and was now stalking the family of her ex-boyfriend.

"I'm . . . uh . . . I'm just taking some time to think." She sounded unconvincing, even to her own ears.

"Are you sure everything is okay?" Curiosity—and maybe some skepticism—stained Austin's voice.

"Yeah, I'm fine. I'm staying out of trouble."

"That's good news. And no signs of danger, right?"

She glanced at the tomb-like house with no signs of life inside. "I'll call you first thing if there are, okay?"

"Thanks. I feel better knowing that."

Skye remembered waking up in his arms. The feel of his heartbeat beneath her ear. The completeness she felt when she was with him. "Austin?"

He paused for a moment. "Yeah?"

Austin what? What was she about to say? That she loved him?

The thought nearly choked her.

Finally, Skye cleared her throat. "How are you feeling today?"

"I'm sore, but okay."

"I'm glad." She hung up, kicking herself for making things awkward. She never had been good at relationships. Maybe not even friendships.

She lowered her phone and stared at the house again.

Sitting here wasn't working.

Skye was going to need to expedite this process and get closer.

Austin nodded at the matching house beside the one he'd been working on, still mulling over the realization that his construction site had been tampered with.

"Maybe I'll go talk to a few of the neighbors," he finally told Wes. "It looks like someone is staying at the house next door. Maybe they saw something."

Austin had come here with the intention of putting his scaffolding back together and finishing the job—with Wes's help. But now that he knew someone had tampered with his equipment, his priorities had shifted.

He could have been killed yesterday. Was that someone's intention? If so, why?

"It can't hurt to talk to a few people." Wes followed his gaze. "Maybe someone even has a security camera."

They walked to where the lane split with one driveway leading to Seagull Palace and the other to the house beside it. Austin checked out the license plates in the driveway as he passed. The people here were from North Carolina. Were they renters? Or had the home-owners come back to use the property?

The house was obviously a rental. A sign on the front

gave the name, Aquaholic, along with a property number and management company name for inquiries.

Austin and Wes climbed the front steps and rang the bell. A moment later, a woman answered. She was older—in her late sixties, probably. And she didn't look like a vacationer, not with her paint-splattered clothes and the half-blue walls beyond her.

"I hate to interrupt you, but my name is Austin Brooks, and I'm working on the house next door," he started.

The woman smiled. "Seagull Palace? Yes, we saw you over there yesterday. I thought about getting your number in case I need some work done on our place. No way either of us is climbing that high to look at the roof."

"I don't blame you. Especially after my day yesterday."

Her smile slipped and creases formed on her brow. "I saw the ambulance, but it was after the accident must have happened. Is everyone okay?"

Austin nodded. "Thankfully, yes."

"I'm Yvonne, by the way. What can I do for you?" The woman shifted her paintbrush to her other hand.

"Listen, I was wondering if you saw anyone over by the house yesterday? Anyone besides me and the ambulance?"

She didn't have to think about it long. "Someone from

the management company was there earlier, before you came."

"The management company?"

Yvonne nodded. "I mean, I assume that's who it was. She was dressed professionally, and she walked around the perimeter of the house like she was inspecting it."

Austin's breath caught. Was this the lead he was looking for? "Did you see her stop by the scaffolding?"

"As a matter of fact, I did. I wondered for a moment if she was going to climb it. She didn't, of course." Yvonne shook her head, like the thought was ludicrous. "Why do you ask? Is everything okay?"

Austin and Wes exchanged a glance. "Someone messed with my equipment and caused the accident."

Yvonne's eyes widened. "I'm sorry to hear that. I can't say for sure that this woman messed with it. She didn't look the type."

"Could you describe her?"

"She had dark hair. Kind of curly. To her shoulders. She was youngish—probably in her early thirties."

Austin froze. Could that be the woman he'd seen on the beach on the day he'd performed the ocean rescue? He presumed she was the mom of the boy he'd rescued. He'd met her briefly at the clinic when he'd gone there to check on the boy that day, and thought her name was Emma.

But why would she be here at his jobsite? It seemed unlikely that she would even know he worked here, so . . . was it just a coincidence?

Austin didn't know the answers. But he didn't like this.

CHAPTER THIRTEEN

SKYE LEFT her bike at the house and hurried down the street and across a sand dune. As she made her way down the beach, she pushed on her sunglasses and pulled her hair back into a bun.

The disguise wasn't great, but at least she might blend in a little better. She climbed atop a lifeguard stand that wasn't in use and sat there, letting the sun warm her face.

As Skye looked out across the beach, her breath caught. Briar was out here.

Someone she didn't recognize—a woman in her late teens or early twenties—kicked a soccer ball with him on the sand.

A nanny, if Skye had to guess. The young woman was probably thirty pounds overweight and didn't look especially athletic. But she was giving the game her best effort.

Skye watched Briar. He looked so happy to be outside. His eyes were lit with excitement. There was a bounce in his steps, and his hair flopped up and down with every stride he took.

Was Briar better off with a family like the Winthrops than he would be with her? Her heart twisted at the question. Mostly because she didn't have an easy answer.

This family could give him everything. And Emma had desperately wanted a child. Maybe things had worked out for the best.

But had Emma taught Briar to appreciate watching the sunset? Or the joy of picking your own fruit and eating it fresh from the vine? Or how delightful it could be to splash in puddles and dance in the rain?

Because those were things money couldn't buy. And they were important things.

Briar missed the soccer ball and began chasing it her way. Skye hopped down from the lifeguard stand and stopped the ball before it rolled past. Reaching down, she grabbed it and extended it toward Briar as he ran her way.

"Here you go."

He paused and squinted against the sun at her. "Hey, you're that woman who came to our door the other day."

"I am. I'm Skye."

"I'm Briar," he reminded her.

"You like playing soccer, Briar?"

"I do. My mom says tennis would be better, but I hate tennis. It's almost as boring as golf."

Skye grinned. He really was a delightful boy. "I agree. Soccer is much more exciting. Have you had fun on your vacation?"

He shrugged. "I don't know. I thought I'd get to spend more time with my mom and dad. But they've been busy doing adult things. Like reading the newspaper and talking. It's a little boring."

"I understand." Skye had played soccer for a couple years in junior high and high school—until her grades had suffered and she'd been forced to quit. "Soccer would be my choice too."

The nanny jogged up to them, out of breath and her cheeks flushed. "Sorry if he's bothering you. He's a talker. Aren't you, Briar? And what have I told you about talking to strangers?"

"She's not a stranger. Besides, you hate soccer, Ruth," Briar called over his shoulder. "At least you don't have to play right now."

Ruth laughed. "I can't argue with that. I'm not much of an athlete."

"I'll kick the ball with you for a moment," Skye said, knowing it was a risky move. But she couldn't pass up the opportunity.

"You will? Yes!" He pulled his arm back in a "victory"

motion.

Briar jogged down the sand. When he was a good distance away, he kicked the ball toward Skye. She kicked it back.

A satisfaction like Skye had never known filled her.

This should have been her life. With her son. Doing simple things.

If she could go back, there were so many things she would have done differently. So. Many. Things.

"What do you think you're doing?" someone growled behind her.

Skye froze and turned.

It was Emma.

And proverbial steam was coming out of her ears as she glared at Skye.

"I'll go talk to the management company," Cassidy said, flipping her notebook shut and turning toward Austin. "If someone tampered with your scaffolding, then we need to investigate."

The police chief had shown up thirty minutes ago, and now Cassidy, Wes, and Austin stood outside the house where Austin had been replacing the shingles. The moldering, earthy scent of the marsh rose around them, and the air had thickened with humidity. Or maybe Austin's heart had just sped as he'd thought about the implications of what he'd learned.

Austin nodded. "Thank you, Cassidy. I appreciate it."

Cassidy pivoted toward him, a knot between her eyebrows. "But I have to say, Austin—whatever is going on here, I don't like it. Why would someone be in Skye's RV last night? Why would they tamper with your jobsite?"

"That's what I'm trying to figure out."

"But you said the person the neighbor described fits the description of the mom of the little boy who almost drowned?"

"That's right. Skye has some kind of connection with the family. She used to date the son."

"You know who they are, right?" Cassidy asked.

Austin shook his head. "Should I?"

"They own Winthrop Cosmetics. They're an empire in the beauty industry."

The news rushed through Austin like a bomb had exploded in his mind. He'd known the family was wealthy —that was obvious. He just hadn't realized they were *that* wealthy.

"Ever since she first saw them on the beach, Skye hasn't been herself," he finally said. "I'm not sure why exactly."

"I'll see what I can find out."

"Thank you," Austin said.

As soon as Cassidy left, Austin turned to Wes. It was already well beyond lunch time. All of this had taken up the majority of the day. The sun had been setting by 6:30, which only gave them a couple more hours of daylight.

"I'm not sure there's much use continuing to work here today," Austin said. "Not only will it be dark soon, but it feels like rain is coming."

Wes looked at the horizon. "Yeah, there's a storm blowing in. You're right."

"Sorry to waste your time." Austin picked up some of his equipment and began to move it onto the deck. If it did storm, the last thing he wanted was for the rain to ruin whatever was salvageable.

Wes began helping him. "You didn't waste my time. But with everything that's happened, are you still going to be able to help me on that kayak tour on Thursday?"

Austin picked up another piece of scaffolding. "That's right. I'd almost forgotten."

"If you're able, I'd still love your help. No way can I manage a bridal party of sixteen all by myself. Not even with Colton helping me."

"I'll be there, then," Austin said.

Wes put another armful of supplies on the deck before glancing at his watch. That was their last load—at least the last load of what they could easily get to today.

"Well, if we're done, I need to go to work for a while," Wes said. "You good?"

Austin nodded. "Yeah, I'm fine. Let me just call Skye and check in with her."

"You're really worried about her, aren't you?"

"Yeah, I am. Especially if the woman who tampered with the job site is Emma Winthrop Harrington."

CHAPTER FOURTEEN

"BRIAR, GO BACK INSIDE," Emma seethed.

"But, Mom! I was having fun—"

"Ruth—take him inside, please. Now." Emma's voice left no room for argument.

The nanny took Briar's arm and led him away, despite his protests. Skye's heart ached at the sight.

Keep that fire inside you, baby boy. It will help you survive later in life, when things get tough.

It was that same fire inside that had helped Skye survive.

As soon as Briar and Ruth disappeared from sight, Emma stepped closer to Skye, beams shooting from her eyes. "What do you think you're doing?"

"I was on the beach." Skye raised her chin, ready to stand her ground. "No crime in that."

Emma narrowed her eyes even more. "Are you stalking us?"

"How can I be stalking you? I live here. You're the ones here for a visit. I should ask you that question."

She raised her hand, shaking her finger at Skye. "Stay away from my son."

"I wasn't doing anything wrong. We were playing soccer." Skye wasn't going to let Emma intimidate her. No, she'd allowed that for far too long.

"I don't care. I don't want trash like you near him."

Skye's cheeks stung, almost as if she'd been slapped. But she didn't dare show it. Emma was trying to shake her up and didn't deserve the satisfaction of thinking she'd succeeded.

"Why are you being so overprotective?" Skye asked, her gaze unwavering. "Is there something you're hiding, Emma?"

"I don't have anything to hide."

"You're acting like it."

Emma leered closer—so close that Skye could feel the spittle shooting from Emma's mouth. "I'm being overprotective because you're nothing but trouble, Skye. You always have been, and you always will be. I don't want you anywhere near my family, especially my son."

The fire inside Skye seemed to grow with every change of this conversation. "The son that you love so much you didn't even notice he was in the ocean and almost drowned."

Emma pulled her hand back and slapped Skye across the face.

Skye reeled, her skin stinging as she brought her own hand over her cheek.

But what she'd said was true. Briar had probably been out there a good twenty or thirty minutes before his family noticed he was even missing.

"My family is none of your business," Emma growled. "And I'm a good mom. Just because I had one lapse in judgment doesn't mean anything. Do you understand me?"

"Well, if it isn't Skye!" A voice cut through the thick, windy air before Skye could retort.

Skye turned and saw Atticus Winthrop tromping through the sand toward her, a friendly smile on his tanned face.

Of everyone in the family, Atticus had always been Skye's favorite. He was warmer than his wife and offspring. Maybe it was because he'd also grown up with nothing, only to create this empire he ran now. Or maybe he was just a good businessman and knew a little kindness could help him get what he wanted.

Skye glanced at Emma and saw her demeanor morph from angry and bitter to the perfect child.

Not much had changed. The woman knew how to transform in order to get what she wanted.

"It's good to see you, Atticus," Skye said.

He reached out his arms and gave her a hug. "I heard you were living here now. Ian told me."

"Small world, huh?"

"You can say that again. We picked this place because we were certain we wouldn't run into anyone we knew." He chuckled. "But you know how that works sometimes."

"I do."

"You still look as beautiful as ever, Skye. It looks like life is finally treating you well."

"I had a few hard years, but things are just starting to work out." She glanced at Emma and saw the woman's skin go a little paler. Skye had chosen her words on purpose. She couldn't let Emma think she was going to tromp into town and start giving Skye orders. No, that wasn't going to happen.

"Listen, why don't you join us for lunch tomorrow?" Atticus asked. "It would be nice to catch up."

"Lunch?" Skye repeated, uncertain if she'd heard correctly. This family had wanted her permanently out of their lives. They'd even gone as far as to pay her off to insure it happened.

"Yes, lunch. At our place."

Skye thought about it for only a moment. Another chance to talk to Briar? It was a no-brainer. "I'd love to."

Atticus smiled. "Great. Come by at one, and we'll have Frank prepare something for all of us."

"Sounds great."

"I look forward to it." Atticus turned to Emma. "Your mother is looking for you. It's time for your massage."

"Of course," Emma muttered.

But the woman threw Skye one more dirty look before following after her father.

CHAPTER FIFTEEN

TEARS TRIED to flood Skye's eyes again as she hurried down the road on her bike. With each moment that passed, she felt more and more certain that Briar was her son. The problem was that she had no way to prove it.

Evening was starting to descend, and Skye hated being out here on her bike in the dim lighting. It wasn't safe, especially when she had no choice but to ride on the main highway through town. There was little shoulder on the side of the road. No, instead there were patches of sand and huge ditches filled to the brim with standing water.

Emma's words echoed in her mind. Skye had brought trouble with her wherever she went when she'd been a teenager. But she'd grown up since then. She'd changed. She knew she had.

Yet that didn't stop the doubts from creeping in.

Maybe Skye *would* be a terrible mother.

One thing felt certain, though. Emma was hiding something. So was Ian.

Was the whole family in on this?

It didn't make sense.

And it only made her want to push harder.

Skye had to know for sure what the truth was. But she had no idea how to go about discovering that. She had so few resources.

Her work brought her fulfillment and built the simple life she'd always wanted. But she was one emergency away from being totally broke.

She pedaled harder.

A fat raindrop hit her on the forehead. Rain? She had no idea it was supposed to rain today.

Just as the thought landed in her mind, the plops became a downpour.

Skye gripped her handlebars tighter. She needed to get back. She could call someone to give her a ride, but by the time they got here to pick her up, she might as well ride back to her camper herself.

She stayed as close to the edge of the road as she could when she saw headlights behind her. An SUV loaded with kayaks on top and bikes on the bike rack slowly went around her.

Not much farther. She only had about a mile to her place. She could get there in five or six minutes if she pushed herself hard enough.

Another car coming toward her blinded her a moment. The headlights were bright against the otherwise dim sky around her.

This had all been a bad idea, hadn't it?

She glanced behind her and saw two more vehicles coming. She braced herself for them to pass. With the rain, it would be harder for them to see her. The reflectors on the back of her bike should help, but they didn't guarantee anything.

The first car passed—a little too fast—but it eased away from the edge of the road to give her space.

Skye flung some wet hair out of her eyes and pushed forward. Thoughts of her conversation with Ian still churned in her mind.

She'd been living under this oppressive weight for a long time—a weight brought on by guilt and shame. Even since becoming a Christian, she hadn't been able to shrug the feelings off. Maybe for a moment or two. But never permanently.

But if people liked her, it needed to be for who she was. Skye was tired of hiding. She needed to tell her friends the truth about her past. If they walked away then they were never really her friends.

It would hurt. But it was better than being around fair-weather relationships. She should have learned that lesson by now.

She glanced behind her again.

She just needed the other car to pass, and then she didn't see any more vehicles. She'd be home free after that.

The car edged closer. She could hear it. Feel it. Or was it an SUV?

It was hard to tell. It appeared to be coming fast, though.

She pulled as close as she could to the edge of the asphalt. She knew if she went off the pavement, she'd crash. There was a good two-inch drop-off between the blacktop and the sand—enough that it could make her fall.

Skye wiped the water from her eyes, desperate to see the road.

She heard the car behind her, getting closer.

Almost here.

The driver would see her and pull toward the center line to pass. It was required by law to share the road with bikers.

She glanced behind her again. The vehicle had almost reached her—but the driver wasn't pulling over to give her space.

Skye sucked in a breath. Did the driver not see her?

She waved a hand in the air, hoping to get his attention.

Just as she did, she felt the car edge closer. Too close

It brushed against her, accelerating as it went past.

She lost control of her bike. It wobbled.

Skye blinked, trying to get the water out of her eyes while gripping the handlebars to maintain control.

But before she could catch herself, she toppled into the sand next to her and heard the gut-wrenching mangle of metal.

Austin barreled down the highway, mentally replaying Skye's frantic phone call over and over again. It had been hard to make out what she was saying between the wind blowing into her phone, the rain, and her obvious anxiety that pitched her voice higher than normal.

All he knew was that there had been accident, and she was okay. She'd asked him to come pick her up.

The windshield wipers on his truck lunged back and forth, pushing the rain out of the way and allowing him to see glimpses into the darkness.

He worried about Skye riding her bike everywhere. He knew it was more cost-efficient than keeping gas in her car, but some of the drivers around here had no common sense and no respect for the speed limit.

The thought burned him up inside.

He held his breath as he reached the area where Skye said she would be.

Austin scanned the highway. Though there were beach houses on either side of the road, most were empty right now. That meant this strip of the streets might as well be abandoned.

There!

He spotted a lone figure standing on the side of the road.

Putting on his flashers, Austin pulled over and jumped out of his truck. He jogged toward Skye and gripped her arms, desperate to see for himself that she was okay.

Her hair clung to her face, and her clothes clung to her skin. She was drenched. But he didn't see any blood or any other signs she'd been injured.

"Are you okay?" he asked, his voice gruff with emotion.

She nodded. "Just shaken."

Austin didn't bother to ask her what happened. Not now. Not out here. Instead, he took her elbow. "Come on. Get in my truck. It's not safe out here."

He waited until she was tucked safely in his cab.

Then he grabbed her bike—a mangled mess, but he wasn't going to leave it—and put it in the back of his truck. He climbed inside and cranked on the heat.

It wasn't cold outside, but Skye was shivering, probably from both being drenched and from adrenaline.

He wished he had a blanket or something else to offer her.

He turned down the stereo until the twang of country music was barely audible in the background. The music was offset by the sound of the windshield wipers slapping water across the glass and the pitter-patter of rain. The sound helped to even out his heart rate.

As much as he'd love to stay here and chat, he needed to get off the road. They could talk later. He did a U-turn and started back to his place, reaching over to squeeze Skye's knee. He left his hand there, and she didn't fight it.

"Are you sure you're okay?" he asked, glancing at her. Had something else happened? Something more than this accident?

Skye nodded, her gaze still vacant. "Yeah, I landed in the sand. I can't say the same for my bike."

"What happened?"

"I was riding back when someone came by too fast. I flew off my bike—and it was a good thing I did. The SUV ran over the tire. I don't even think the driver realized he hit me."

Austin wasn't so sure about that. His scaffolding accident, and now this? It was too early to jump to any conclusions, but he didn't like two "coincidences" like that happening two days in a row.

And it was right after this new family from Skye's past rolled into town.

"I know I shouldn't have been out," Skye said. "It was too wet. That storm popped up out of nowhere."

"You can always call me if you need me."

"I know. I do. And I appreciate that. I just thought I could make it."

Austin pulled to a stop at his place. Maybe it had been presumptuous to bring her back here. But he needed to know she was okay.

He climbed out of the truck and hurried around to help Skye out. As she slid to the ground, he took her hand. They ran toward his porch, but Skye put on brakes before they reached the steps.

He paused and turned toward her, worried something was wrong. To his surprise, she closed her eyes and let the rain hit her face.

What in the world was she doing?

She didn't seem to be in distress. No, she actually looked at peace, like the rain was washing away her worries and fears.

"Skye?"

She opened her eyes, and her gaze met his. There was something new there. Conviction? Determination?

He wasn't sure.

"I mess up things, Austin," she murmured.

"We've all messed up." Where was she going with this?

"No, I have a track record," she shouted over the rain. "It's usually my fault."

He squinted as moisture from above poured into his eyes. "Do you want to go inside and talk?"

Skye raked her hair out of her eyes and stared up at him with big, expressive eyes that said more than words could. "If I go inside with you, I'm going to kiss you."

Austin's heart rate surged. Had he just heard her correctly? "Is that a bad thing?"

Something electric zipped through her gaze, and she stepped closer. "I don't know. Is it?"

Austin met her in one stride and pulled her into his arms. His gaze went to her lips. Her full, plump lips. Her lithe body. Her long hair that was now plastered to her neck.

His throat went dry. Skye was so beautiful. So, so beautiful. Inside and out. And she didn't even realize it.

Skye's arms slipped around his neck, and she tugged him closer.

That was all the invitation Austin needed.

Their lips met tentatively—but only for a couple seconds. Then Austin pulled Skye closer, locking his arms around her waist. Her breath caught for only a second before her arms tugged him even closer.

The kiss deepened, and all the pent-up passion they had for each other escaped into one blissful, rain-soaked moment.

When they finally pulled away, Austin knew the dopey smile on Skye's face matched his own.

"Do you have any idea how long I've wanted to do that?" he murmured, running his thumb across her jaw.

"Me too."

"Then why haven't we?"

Skye nibbled her bottom lip and shrugged. "I've been too scared. But when you almost died in that accident . . . and then my accident tonight . . . I just realized there's no time to be scared. We might not be here tomorrow, and I'd hate for you not to know how I felt about you. I'm tired of living in fear."

Pure delight rippled through his heart. "So am I."

Skye's grip on him loosened a moment, and she stepped back. "There are things we should talk about, Austin."

Yes, there were things they needed to talk about. Austin needed to tell her the truth about his past and how he'd been struggling lately with choices made on his behalf as a child. Skye needed to know the hurt he wrestled with, and why those hurts had him keeping her at arm's length for so long.

"Let's get inside." Austin wrapped his arm around Skye, never wanting to let her go. "And we need to call Cassidy and tell her what happened."

CHAPTER SIXTEEN

SKYE SAT cross-legged on Austin's couch and sipped some coffee he'd fixed. She'd pulled her wet hair up into a sloppy bun and had changed into an old flannel shirt and sweats belonging to Austin while her clothes dried.

Cassidy was coming in two hours. She had to wrap up a dispute between two neighbors, and she wanted to come herself instead of sending Officer Quinton.

It was just as well.

She and Austin had a lot to talk about.

Austin sat beside her, his wavy hair falling into his face. He was gorgeous. Handsome. Honorable.

Everything she could ever want.

Did she dare hope . . . ?

She sucked on her bottom lip. That kiss had been amazing. Beyond amazing. And her heart felt like it might burst right now. But before she could relish the moment, she had to tell him the truth.

Austin's arm stretched along the back of the couch, and he focused his full attention on her. "I'm glad you want to talk because I have something I want to tell you also."

"You go first." Was this about his secret project?

He glanced down at his hands and drew in a long, deep breath before looking at her again. "There's a part of my past that I don't open up about very often, Skye. Honestly, it's too painful."

"I know what that's like." Despite her casual words, Skye braced herself for what he had to say.

Austin took her hand and rubbed the top of her knuckles, not saying anything for a moment. "The truth is that my mom abandoned me when I was six."

Skye's stomach dropped at his news. "What?"

He nodded, looking somber and almost stoic. This was hard for him. She could tell it was.

"Before you feel too sorry for me, I should add that I had a wonderful family adopt me when I was eight."

"Well, that's good. But . . . what . . . what happened? What do you mean, your mom abandoned you?"

He squeezed her hand again and leaned back, his eyes looking distant, like he'd gone back in time to another world—and a painful one, at that. "My mom was a single mom, trying hard to make ends meet on her own. We had some really great memories together when I was little. When she was having a good day, she'd make pillow forts with me and we'd race paper airplanes and see who could walk the longest with books piled on top of our heads. But the truth is that my childhood was a struggle. My dad . . . well, I'm not even sure my mom knows who my dad is, if you know what I mean."

Skye nodded, hardly able to breathe. This conversation had shifted things inside her. The truth began to squeeze out her happy feelings. And . . .

She just needed to listen to what else he had to say. *Don't jump to conclusions, Skye. Just give the gift of listening.*

"She worked hard but only earned minimum wage," Austin continued. "We lived in a small, dumpy apartment because that's all we could afford. But all of that changed when she met Travis."

Skye had a feeling this was where the story would take a bad turn. She could hear it in the wispy tone of Austin's voice.

"Travis was wealthy—at least, he acted like he was. And he thought the world of my mom. Took her out for fancy dinners. Bought her gifts. He showed her a whole new life."

"There's a 'but' coming, isn't there?" Skye knew there

was something not so great about this. Somewhere along the line, things had gone terribly wrong, and a little boy's life had been changed forever.

"The problem was that Travis didn't want kids." Austin pulled his hand away from Skye's and raked it through his hair.

She instantly missed his touch. Craved it. But she gave him the space he silently asked for.

"Travis didn't like me," Austin continued. "He merely tolerated me. In the end, he apparently gave my mom an ultimatum. It was me or him."

Skye sucked in a deep breath as she absorbed his words. "No . . ."

Austin nodded. "I came home from school one day, and she wasn't there. That wasn't unusual. She worked long hours. But she never came home that night. I was little. And I was scared. But I didn't call the police. No, I kept thinking she'd come back. But she wasn't home by the next morning. I stayed home from school waiting for her. She still never came. Finally, I went to the neighbors, and they called the police."

"What happened?" Her mind raced ahead, filling in the blanks with terrible, unfathomable things.

"My mom was gone," Austin said. "She'd taken her things and left with Travis. She didn't even have the nerve to tell me goodbye. Of course, I didn't understand all of that at the time. In fact, I didn't understand it until I was about thirteen when she showed up again and begged for my forgiveness. At that point, I'd already been through the foster-care system. And, like I said, I'd been adopted into a great home. But a boy doesn't forget being abandoned by his mom."

"No, I'd imagine he doesn't." Skye's head swam, and she reached for Austin's hand. He didn't pull away.

"She asked for my forgiveness that day, but I wouldn't give it to her. She left crying. And I didn't even care. Not really. There's not one single part of me that can justify someone leaving their child like that. On purpose."

Her head swam even more as the implications of his statement resounded in her head. "I understand."

Finally, Austin's gaze met hers. "But I've decided I need to talk to her again."

Skye's heart skipped a beat as she processed his words. "Why?"

"I don't know." Austin shrugged. "I just know I need to see her. I've been looking for her for the last month, but I haven't been able to locate her. That's what those phone calls have been about. I've hired a PI to help me locate her, and he calls me sporadically to give updates."

"I see. Thank . . . thank you for sharing that and opening up to me."

Austin ran his finger across Skye's cheek, stroking it

gently as he stared at her. "I felt bad keeping it from you. It's a piece of my heart, I suppose. I don't talk about it often. But it's important that I share it with you because . . . well, because you mean the world to me, Skye."

She squeezed his hand harder. He said that now. But how would he feel when she told him the truth?

An ache formed in her chest.

"I hope you find her," Skye finally whispered, her voice cracking with emotion.

"I do too. I need closure." Austin paused for long enough to stare at her, pressing his lips together in thought before saying, "Your turn. What did you want to tell me?"

How could Skye tell him the truth now? That she'd also abandoned her child—just as his mom had. This was a bad idea. All of her hopes that they might have a future together seemed to fizzle.

Skye had been a fool to ever hope at all.

Shouldn't she have learned that lesson by now?

Good things didn't happen to girls like her.

Before she could formulate an excuse and run, Austin's phone buzzed and his eyes narrowed.

"That's weird," he muttered.

"What's weird?"

"I have this alarm system that I installed. I just got a notice that one of my windows just opened."

Skye's back stiffened. "What?"

Austin stood. "Let me check things out. Stay here. Okay?"

She nodded. "Be careful. Please."

As she watched Austin walk to the back of the house, she wondered if this was her chance to flee, to get out of here before she saw the disappointment in Austin's eyes.

Because it just might be more than she could bear.

Austin checked each of the windows but saw nothing. Maybe this system was malfunctioning. Again.

He paused by the window in his bathroom. It was cracked open ever-so-slightly. But as he peered outside, he saw nothing.

Maybe it had just come unlatched. That was probably it.

He shoved it down and locked it again.

As he returned to the living room, he paused.

Where was Skye?

The couch where she'd sat was empty and—

"I got some more coffee." Skye walked back into the room with two mugs in her hands. "I refilled yours also."

Relief washed through him. Austin had thought Skye left or that something had happened. Maybe he was wound a little too tightly right now.

He took the mug from her. "Thank you."

Skye set down the mugs before lowering herself to the couch again. "Everything okay?"

"I must have forgotten to latch my bathroom window. I didn't see anything."

"That's good." She looked up, her gaze veiled by her eyelashes and a noticeable heaviness about her.

What had changed? Why was she pulling away and transforming from the warm woman who'd kissed him like she'd meant it to this woman who held him at a distance?

Austin didn't want to let that happen.

He scooted closer and lowered his voice. They'd been making such progress. But now . . . "Hey, what's wrong?"

He wanted to see that joy he'd seen in her eyes earlier. Wanted to see her walls coming down. He wanted to talk about the two of them as a couple. Together. For what he hoped would be a long time. Forever, actually.

But something had shifted in Skye when Austin told her about his past, and he wasn't sure what or why.

"My first instinct right now is to run," she started, lifting her head slightly. "I don't want you to change your opinion of me. I don't want to see the disappointment in your gaze."

"I would never change my opinion of you." What secret could possibly hold this kind of power over her?

Skye's eyes made it clear she didn't believe his words,

that she fought some kind of inner demon that rocked her world. "Austin . . ."

"You can tell me anything, Skye." He reached for her, resting his hand on her knee.

She rubbed her lips together. Looked at her lap. Finally looked up, but fear was written all across her features.

What Austin wouldn't do to erase that.

"I was at a bad place in my life also, Austin," she started. "My mom kicked me out when I was sixteen. I moved in with a friend, but her dad hit on me. I ran away from that too, got a minimum-wage job, and lived out of a dirt-cheap hotel while I tried to finish high school. I got my GED instead."

Austin's heart ached at the thought of everything she'd been through.

"That's when I met Ian. He came into the restaurant where I worked, and he came in every night until I said yes to a date with him."

"How many nights did that take?"

"Twenty-six."

Austin's eyebrows flickered up. "Wow. He was really pursuing you."

"He was. And we started dating. He was from one of the wealthiest families in the area, and I was from nothing. We both had a rebellious side that got us in trouble."

"What kind of trouble?"

She frowned. "The bad kind of trouble. Ian . . . well, he felt untouchable because of who his family was. And me . . . well, I just didn't have much to live for, I suppose. I knew we needed to break up before . . . well, before one of us died. Before I could, I found out I was pregnant."

Austin sucked in a sharp breath. Pregnant? Skye?

He tried to put the pieces together but reminded himself to slow down. He just needed to finish listening to her tell the story instead of trying to fill in the gaps himself.

As if something in her subconscious had taken over, Skye's hand went to her stomach—now flat. But it was like she'd gone back in time.

"Ian's parents convinced me to give the baby up for adoption," she told him. "I didn't want to. But I had no money. They told me if I went ahead with their plan, they'd give me fifty thousand dollars. I just had to promise to get out of their lives for good."

Austin clenched his hands into fists. The whole thing sounded slimy. "What did Ian say about that?"

"He went along with whatever his parents wanted. He was almost old enough to tap into his trust fund, so I'm sure he didn't want to ruin that." She glanced at her hands again. "I didn't feel like I had any choice. And . . . I believed the lies they told me. I believed I'd be a horrible mom."

Austin grabbed her hand and squeezed it, but Skye pulled away. "Thank you for sharing that, Skye. I know it wasn't easy."

Moisture filled her eyes. "And now you know why we won't work together, no matter how much either of us wants it."

He flinched. "What do you mean? Our pasts are our pasts, Skye."

"You'll never look at me the same, Austin."

"Skye—"

She stood before he could grab her hand again.

"It's true," she continued. "I abandoned my baby just like your mom abandoned you. You deserve so much better."

"It was different. You didn't leave your child without explanation so you could run off with some guy. You were trying to be responsible, even if Ian's family manipulated you."

"No, it wasn't different!" Her voice climbed. She sucked in a breath and closed her eyes. "What kind of person am I to give my child up?"

He tamped down the emotion in his voice. "It was a brave choice, Skye."

"No, I was a coward. I didn't want to stand up to Ian's family."

"You were young."

"But in my gut, I knew what I should have done. You might not resent me now, Austin, but you will. You'll realize that I'm the kind of person who'd give up the people I love for an easier life. All of those feelings you have about your mom will become feelings you direct at me. It's only natural."

"You can't know that."

Her tortured, red-rimmed eyes met his. "But I do."

"So you're just going to end this before it even starts? You're going to make the decision for me?"

"I don't even know if this is really about you, Austin. Maybe you can forgive me. But can I ever forgive myself?"

Before Austin could respond, a knock sounded on the door. Cassidy was here to take Skye's statement on the bike incident.

He was going to have to save the rest of this conversation for later.

But his heart felt like it had twisted so tightly that it might break.

CHAPTER SEVENTEEN

SKYE SAW Cassidy glance at her clothes in confusion.

"I got wet and Austin let me borrow some dry clothes," she explained, looking down at her oversized sweats and flannel shirt.

Cassidy raised a hand. "No judgment. Just not your normal look."

Skye felt like she'd just been run over. And, in a way, she had—both physically and emotionally. She had no idea sharing her story with Austin would be so draining.

She'd also had no idea things would take this turn. But she knew she had to tell Austin the truth. He had to know why they would be so wrong together. Why their kiss was only a moment of bliss, but that it could never last a lifetime . . . even if that was what Skye's heart truly desired.

"So what's going on?" Cassidy pulled up a chair and sat across from them at the dining room table.

Ty had come with her and also pulled up a chair. "Do you mind if I stay? Mac and I are unofficially giving her a hand until she hires someone else."

"Not at all," Skye said.

Skye made sure to put distance between her and Austin. Based on the way her gaze slid back and forth between them, Cassidy seemed to notice that also. Then again, she noticed everything.

Skye told Cassidy about the person who'd nearly run her over.

"Is this connected with the scaffolding incident?" Cassidy asked.

"What do you mean?" Skye glanced at Austin. She knew about his accident, but Cassidy made it sound like there was more to it.

"Someone tampered with my jobsite," Austin finally said.

"What?" Why hadn't she heard about this yet?

"We just discovered it today. I was going to mention it, but other matters seemed more pressing . . ."

"Oh, Austin. Why?" And why did things keep going from bad to worse?

He shook his head. "I don't know."

Could someone really have done that on purpose? Skye didn't want to believe it.

But there was one other detail she needed to share.

Skye cleared her throat. "There is one more thing I need to mention."

Everyone's attention riveted toward her.

There was one part of the story that Skye hadn't gotten to when she was talking to Austin: the events that had happened since Ian arrived in town.

"The little boy Austin rescued yesterday . . ." Skye started, her cheeks hot with emotion. "He's the same age as my son would have been."

"What?" Austin's voice cracked with surprise.

"Your son?" Cassidy asked, her forehead furrowed.

Skye gave her a quick breakdown.

"Did you ask Ian about Briar?" Austin said, looking slightly dazed. Anyone would.

Skye nodded. "I did. He claims Briar is an in vitro baby, born six months after I left. I just know he looks like me."

"Okay, I'm going to get back to that in a minute." Cassidy tapped her pen against her chin. "Is there a chance that this family is behind what happened today?"

Skye licked her lips before rubbing them together in thought. "I don't know. I mean . . . I guess. But why would they target Austin?"

"Maybe to distract you from the truth," Cassidy suggested.

"But how would they even know where Austin was or what he was doing?" Skye just couldn't believe this. The family might be ruthless, but they wouldn't take things his far . . . would they?

"I went to visit them at the clinic and ran into one of the guys who works with me sometimes," Austin said, his voice thin and dull. "They could have overheard me talking to him. I was telling him about the house."

"They wouldn't . . ." But Skye couldn't finish the statement. She knew the truth.

The Winthrops would do whatever they could to get whatever they wanted.

"What do I do, Cassidy?" Skye searched her friend's face, desperate for answers.

"From what you've told me, they didn't commit a crime when they talked you into giving the baby up. It sounds like everything was done legally, and you were over eighteen. If Ian's sister did adopt your baby, there's nothing criminal about that—unless they cut corners somewhere. From the sounds of it, this family is very thorough."

"So I can't do anything? I just have to take their word for it?" Skye's voice climbed in pitch as her emotions rose.

"You can go through the court system and petition for

a blood test maybe. But that takes time and money. You won't get quick results."

"I won't get results at all. I don't have that kind of money." Skye remembered Jimmy James's offer.

No, she couldn't even think about that. Unless she could do this legally, she wouldn't do it at all. In her old life, she hadn't had much of a moral compass. But now she did.

"And if it was a closed adoption . . ." Cassidy's voice trailed off, and she frowned as if she didn't like the conclusions she drew. "I don't know, Skye. I'll see what I can find out. I can question the family and see if their vehicle matches the description of the one that ran you off the road. I can look for scrapes or other evidence. Maybe we can nab them on other charges until we figure this out."

"What about Austin? Did they try to hurt him?" Skye didn't dare look at him for fear of turning into a puddle of emotions.

Hurting her was one thing. But hurting the people she cared about? Skye couldn't handle that.

"Again, I don't know. We're trying to figure out those answers. In the meantime, don't take matters into your own hands here. Promise me."

Cassidy leveled her gaze with her until Skye nodded. "Okay."

"Is Serena in town?"

Skye shook her head. "No, she went to another wedding. This one's down in Florida. She's becoming bridesmaid of the year."

"You shouldn't stay alone. You want to come to my place?"

"She can stay here." Austin's voice cut through the room, strong and firm and leaving little room for argument. "She can stay upstairs, I'll stay on the couch. Scouts' honor."

"You don't have to do that." Being around Austin was torture, especially since all she wanted to do was kiss him again.

"I insist. I won't forgive myself if something happens to you."

"But . . ."

"It's a good idea, Skye," Ty said. "Until we have answers, you need to play it safe."

Finally, Skye nodded, knowing she wasn't going to win here, not when all of her friends were in agreement. It wasn't worth the energy of fighting over it. "Okay, then. But hopefully this will be resolved soon, and I won't have to worry all of you."

"We're your friends, Skye," Cassidy said. "We're supposed to worry about you."

"Even knowing my past?" Skye hardly wanted to hear her answer.

Cassidy and Ty exchanged a glance before Cassidy licked her lips and turned to her.

"We all have secrets in our past, Skye," Cassidy said. "We just can't let the past define us."

Austin looked over at Skye after Cassidy and Ty left. There were a million things he wanted to say to her, but instead awkwardness shifted between them.

She had a child. A child she'd given up for adoption because she thought he would have a better life without her. It had been a brave choice, and it wasn't nearly the same thing his mom had done to him.

But could Austin make Skye see that? Could he make her see that he didn't think any less of her? Or would their pasts form a wedge between them?

This was not the result he'd imagined would happen. He'd thought the revelation about his own mom would pull them closer together. Instead, it had driven them apart. Far apart.

He stood, sensing that Skye needed space. "I'll get the bedroom ready for you."

Skye stood also with her arms crossed and a strangely vacant look in her eyes. Finally she nodded. "Thank you."

Austin began changing the sheets, turning things over in his mind.

Maybe legally that adoption had been okay. But from a moral perspective, the Winthrop family had practically coerced Skye into signing those papers. And they'd most likely done so with their own agenda in mind.

It was wrong.

But Cassidy was correct when she'd said there might be nothing they could do about it. Skye could go to court, but it would be a lengthy and expensive process. Skye couldn't afford that.

Austin finished changing the sheets and lumbered back down the stairs. Skye was still in the same position, with her arms crossed and that withdrawn look on her face. Austin wanted to take her into his arms and promise her that everything would be okay.

But he couldn't do that.

"Skye?" he started.

Her gaze flickered up to his.

"What are you thinking?" he asked.

"That I need space to process everything. I imagine you do too."

"Above all, we're still friends, right?"

Surprise raced through her gaze.

"You're my best friend." Her voice cracked.

"And nothing's going to change that, okay? Not that

kiss. Not awkward conversations. Not revelations about the past."

Though he would desperately like to recreate that kiss —that amazing, amazing kiss.

"You mean that?" Skye stared up at him, her voice cracking as if she didn't dare believe him.

He squeezed her arm. "Of course I do. I'll always be there for you."

Finally, a tentative smile flickered across her face. "That means a lot, Austin. Thank you."

"Of course."

She nodded to the loft. "If it's okay, I'm going to turn in. I'm exhausted, and I have a lot to think about. Too much."

He started to reach for her but dropped his arm. "Good night, Skye."

"Good night, Austin."

CHAPTER EIGHTEEN

AT SIX A.M., Skye finally pulled her eyes open. She hadn't gotten much sleep last night—hardly any, truth be told. Between reviewing everything that had happened and getting wisps of Austin's aftershave from the sheets, she'd been doomed to a sleepless night.

She heard a gentle clanging downstairs that indicated Austin was already awake. And based on the aroma that drifted upward, he was cooking.

Cooking.

When was the last time someone had cooked for her?

She pressed her face back into the pillow. Why did she have to meet someone like Austin? Someone who showed her just how good life might be if she hadn't messed up beyond repair?

A memory of their kiss filled her thoughts. It had been

. . . fantastic. Better than she could have imagined. Yet to hope for more of that in her life would be foolish.

Every time Austin looked at her, he would be reminded that Skye was the same kind of person as his mother. She'd given up her baby in exchange for a new life for herself.

A small cry escaped from her at the thought.

If Skye could go back, there were so many things she would have done differently. But wishing for those things was futile. She'd made her choices, and now she had to live with the consequences for the rest of her life. She pulled back the tears that tried to burn her eyes. Crying would do no good.

Finally, she threw the covers off, knowing she needed to face the music. Skye made herself as presentable as she could—her clothes had dried, so at least there was that—and she went downstairs.

Austin either didn't hear her or didn't turn. Which gave Skye the chance to watch him a minute. He stood at the stove, expertly going back and forth between a skillet of bacon and a pan of scrambled eggs. His broad back was toward her, muscles rippling beneath the thin fabric of his T-shirt.

All of those hours of physical labor had paid off, and his physique showed it. It wasn't the inorganic kind of muscle. No, his build could wholly be attributed to the fact that he was doing what he loved to do. It fit him.

And that was just one more thing Skye loved about him.

Finally, Austin looked over his shoulder at her. "I thought I heard you stirring. Morning."

And there he went. Being so kind. But there had to be a part of him that resented her. No matter what he said, Skye knew that must be true.

"Good morning." She stood beside him. "Can I help with anything?"

He nodded toward some apples that he'd bought from her stand earlier in the week. "Could you chop a few of those?"

"Of course." They were her favorite kind. Winesaps, straight from a grower in the mountains.

Austin helped her find a cutting board and knife, and Skye began working. As she did, her thoughts lingered on what Lisa had said. Was it true that Austin didn't even like fruits or vegetables?

The thought shouldn't delight her so much. But it did.

After she finished chopping the Winesaps, Austin plated the eggs and bacon, and they sat down at a small table.

"Do you mind if I flip on the news?" he asked.

"I thought Wes was the news junkie."

Austin shrugged. "I watch it in the morning just to catch the weather usually."

"I suppose that's kind of important for your work. Absolutely, turn it on."

A local station came on the small screen, creating somewhat of a static noise in the background.

At once, visions of doing this forever filled her.

Don't be a fool, Skye. You and Austin would never work.

The words from the newscaster caught her ear. Skye forgot about her food and turned toward the screen.

The reporter faced the camera. "In other news, rumor has it that Atticus Winthrop will soon announce his candidacy for US Senate. Winthrop has been active in philanthropy in North Carolina for years, serving on the board of numerous charities . . ."

Skye's stomach churned, her appetite suddenly gone. It would be hard enough fighting someone as wealthy as the Winthrops. But fighting someone in a position of power also?

The task felt impossible.

Austin was still trying to comprehend just how powerful

and wealthy this Winthrop family was when a knock sounded at his door. Cassidy stood on the other side.

"May I come in?" Cassidy asked.

"Of course."

Cassidy stepped inside, wearing her police uniform. She might appear professional, but her gaze still held that compassionate look that made it clear she was a friend.

"I'm sorry to stop by so early. I was up all night doing some research." Cassidy's gaze flickered to the TV. "What's this?"

"It appears Atticus is running for office," Skye said. "There are rumors he's going to announce his candidacy soon."

"Isn't that interesting?" Cassidy shook her head, not looking entirely happy with the news.

"Did you find out anything?" Austin nodded toward a chair at the table. "Want some breakfast?"

"No, I'm fine, but thank you." Cassidy sat across from them. "I'll take some coffee if you have some."

Austin poured her a cup and noticed that neither he nor Skye had touched their food. Maybe everyone's appetite was gone. He knew his was.

"I can confirm what I told you last night," Cassidy said. "If you signed away your rights and this was a closed adoption, then there's nothing legally that the Winthrops have done wrong. Are they deplorable for manipulating the situation for their own gain? Absolutely. But legally, there's nothing criminal."

Austin nodded in acknowledgement. He'd figured that much, even though it seemed incredibly unfair.

"I drove past their place, and I didn't see any vehicles matching the description of the one you said ran you off the road," she said. "While they slept, I also checked those vehicles for scratches. There were none."

Austin glanced at Skye and saw her frown.

"Does that mean they didn't do this?" Skye asked.

"Not necessarily. But, if they did, they're good at covering their tracks." Cassidy pressed her lips together, obviously taking this situation seriously. "I can talk to the Winthrops, but I have a feeling they won't be forthcoming."

"They won't be," Skye said.

"However, at least it will let them know that we're not naïve small-town nobodies around here," Cassidy continued. "It will put some pressure on them and let them know we're keeping an eye on them. Maybe they won't try any more stunts like that."

"If you think that will work," Austin said.

"From what you've told me, several members of the family have motive."

Skye nodded. "They do. Emma doesn't want to lose her son. Atticus and Ginger don't want to lose their reputation and political aspirations. They have a security team that can do their dirty work for them."

"What about Ian?" Cassidy's gaze fell on Skye.

"I don't really know what he would have to gain by keeping me quiet," Skye said. "He doesn't really care about his reputation, and he obviously doesn't want to be a father."

"I'll see if I can find anything out. In the meantime, you should be careful, Skye," Cassidy continued. "Until we know what's going on, I'm not sure you're safe. And now that we're hearing about this guy's political aspirations, we know what the stakes are. If something like this becomes public, his election results could be seriously diminished."

"I just don't want to sit back and do nothing."

"I wouldn't suggest talking to them anymore," Cassidy said. "Not for now. And not if they're as manipulative as you say. They'll twist around anything you do."

The hollow feeling in Austin's gut grew. Cassidy was right. Some people would stop at nothing to get what they wanted. The question was: which member of the Winthrop family was that desperate?

CHAPTER NINETEEN

AUSTIN WATCHED as Skye grabbed her purse as soon as Cassidy left.

"I should get home," she muttered.

Austin's back went rigid as he realized what she was doing. "You're still planning on having lunch with the Winthrops, aren't you? Even after all of this?"

A blush raced across her cheeks, but she held her chin high. "I want to see Briar again."

He reached out to her, desperate to get her attention and to make her see the truth—the truth that this was dangerous. That it wasn't a game. But Austin knew by the look of determination in Skye's eyes that she wouldn't back down. No, she desperately wanted answers.

"There's got to be a better way," Austin finally said.

Skye swung her head back and forth, leaving no room

for doubt. "There's not any. Not that I can think of. This family is untouchable. This is my chance to see on the inside."

"Take me with you." His words hung in the air, and he waited with baited breath for her reaction.

She swallowed hard but kept her gaze steady. "I can't do that."

"Skye . . ."

She rested her hand on his chest, her shoulders softening ever so slightly. "Austin, I'm sure you have other things to do. You have a life outside all of this. The Winthrops—you don't want to get on their bad side. They could ruin your life. All they have to do is say the word."

He had no doubt her words were true. "You're more important than any of those jobs."

She smiled softly, her eyes filling with emotion. "I appreciate that. I do. But I've got to do this alone. I'm sorry."

Austin had figured she would say that. But he wasn't done pleading his case yet. "At least, let me drive you. Let me keep an eye on things, just in case you need help."

Indecision raced through Skye's gaze. "They're too smart to hurt me in their house."

"Desperate people will do desperate things."

She seemed to consider his words for a minute before

finally nodding. "Okay, fine. You can drive me. You can wait outside. But I've got to do this by myself."

An hour later, Austin pulled up to the Winthrop's rental house. Skye glanced over at him, her emotions clashing inside her. Part of her wanted to reach over and kiss him, and the other part of her wanted to run.

Instead of dealing with that now, she just needed to figure out this other part of her life. She hoped today might provide some answers.

"Be safe," Austin said, his voice sounding as hoarse as his gaze was strained.

"I will be. Thank you."

Tension pulled between them. Before Skye could question it too much, she opened her door and stepped out. One problem at a time, she reminded herself.

She brushed her hair back from her face as she walked up to the front door. Ginger Winthrop answered, the cold smile on her face as lifeless as her signature pearls.

"Skye, so glad you could make it." Her words sounded nowhere near sincere.

"Thanks for having me." She stepped inside the huge house, trying not to gape at the fancy decorations. But the place was impressive with its driftwood-colored floors, leather couches, and no-expense-spared decorations.

"Ms. Skye, Ms. Skye!" a little voice said. Briar appeared around the corner. "I heard you were coming."

"Hey, you." Skye felt her whole face glow with delight every time she saw him. "How are you today?"

"I'm bored again. Want to play sand soccer?"

"Now, Briar, we're all having lunch together," Ginger scolded. "Give the nice woman some space."

Nice woman. Had Ginger chosen those words on purpose to put Skye in her place? To make her sound like a stranger?

Briar frowned. "Maybe later."

Skye smiled again. "Yes, maybe later."

"Can I go show you the lazy river in the back yard?" he continued.

Skye glanced at Ginger, who looked irritated. Finally, the woman nodded. "I suppose that can't hurt anything."

Briar grabbed her hand and pulled her inside. Skye could hardly keep up. He finally stopped on the other side of the house, opened a sliding glass door, and pulled her outside.

"There it is. Look at it."

Skye's eyes widened. The backyard was a sight to behold. A swimming pool glimmered with turquoise-colored water. A lazy river stretched around it. A few putting greens to the side. Beyond all of that was the Atlantic Ocean.

"It looks perfect, Briar," she told him.

"Maybe you could come try it sometime."

Skye looked down at him and smiled again. "Maybe."

"I forgot to take my raft out of the pool. I've got to go get it. Be right back!"

And as quickly as Briar had led her outside, he was gone.

Someone else stepped up behind her. "He likes you."

Skye turned and saw Ian standing there. "I like him too."

He leaned on the railing, looking a little stiff for Ian. "This lunch may not be as fun as my father thinks it will."

"Your sister pretty much hates me."

"I wish I could deny it."

"It makes me think she's keeping secrets from me."

"I warned you—you shouldn't push it."

"Why? Because you're hiding something?"

Ian pressed his lips together. "Because life is complicated. My family is used to getting what they want, and they don't want anyone to mess that up."

Ian's words caused a coolness to spread across Skye's chest.

"But don't worry. I've got your back." Ian grabbed her hand.

Skye pulled away. "You won't even answer my questions."

"There's nothing to answer. Just because you're speculating, doesn't mean there's any truth to be found. But accusations can ruin a person's life."

His words hung in the air.

"There you are!" Atticus appeared around the corner. "It's time to eat. Skye, we're so glad you could join us. Now, come on before the tuna gets cold."

She followed them to a large dining table that probably seated eighteen people. Emma sat there, her husband again absent. He apparently hadn't joined her on this vacation. Ian sat beside Emma, and Briar at one end of the table along with Atticus and Ginger Winthrop.

It was the perfect setup for an awkward conversation.

Before they even could start to chitchat, food was served, and everyone began digging in. Skye tried to lose herself in the scent of grilled peppers, a spring salad with a citrus vinaigrette, and the savory grilled tuna.

"So, Skye, tell us what you've been up to," Atticus said.

Skye drew in a deep breath, almost regretting coming here.

But this would be worth it if Skye got answers to her questions.

And if she made it out of here alive.

CHAPTER TWENTY

"I RUN A PRODUCE STAND," Skye answered. Why did that answer feel so shameful around such an ambitious, successful family? There was no shame in doing what you loved. Yet she almost felt embarrassed.

Everyone stared at her blankly.

"A produce stand," Atticus finally said. "How quaint."

"It's a simple life, but I like it." Skye cleared her throat. "How about you? I heard a rumor you're running for office."

"That's right. It's something I've always wanted to do. I'll be officially announcing my candidacy soon."

Skye wiped her mouth with her linen napkin, hardly tasting any of her food. "How about your company?"

"We've been training Ian for years to take over. I trust it will all be in good hands if I have to step down one day."

"That's great, then." Skye lifted her water goblet and took a sip, trying not to show her nerves.

"I think fruit is yummy. Can I help you run the stand?" Briar stared at her from the other side of the table. "That sounds fun. Not as fun as soccer, though."

Her heart pounded. This boy . . . he seemed to share so much of her heart.

Skye couldn't be wrong about all this, could she? Briar must be her son. This family had tricked her.

And now she was sitting here, eating with them like nothing had transpired eight years ago.

She held her outrage at bay. The best way to get through this was to keep the upper hand and not let her emotions get the best of her. But she wasn't leaving here without asking some hard questions.

Austin sat in his truck, his mind racing.

What was going on in there?

He didn't know. And he couldn't know. Even if Skye needed his help, Austin would be hard-pressed to figure it out.

Skye might have a son.

That hadn't fully sunk in yet. Nor had it sunk in how that might change Skye's life.

She'd lived with a lot of guilt for a lot of years. That was a heavy burden to carry.

No wonder she'd looked so untrusting. Everyone had let her down.

Austin didn't want to be that kind of person.

His phone rang, and he looked at the screen.

It was Jon Tibbetts, the private investigator he'd hired. His heart rate kicked up a notch as he put the phone to his ear.

"I've got good news," Tibbetts said.

"I could use some good news."

"I found your mom."

Everything else seemed to fade from around him for a minute. "And?"

"And . . . she's working as a cosmetologist in Georgia. She divorced her third husband about five years ago. No other children. Lives in an apartment by herself."

"Is that right?" Austin searched for the right words, the right reaction. He wasn't sure what those things were, though.

"Do you want me to approach her? See if she wants to meet with you or talk to you on the phone?"

He stared out the window another moment. This was it. The moment he'd been waiting for. A reckoning of sorts, and a chance to make things right.

So why did he hesitate? Why did the thought of talking to her again cause him to pause?

So much history stretched between them. He knew it was time to put that history to rest. Despite that, he found himself saying, "Give me a day to think about it. I want to be certain of my decision."

"Okay. I'll wait to hear from you."

After a mostly strained conversation during lunch, everyone finally finished eating. The tension across Skye's shoulders grew with every second that passed.

Maybe she shouldn't have come.

But she wasn't going to leave here knowing only what she had when she'd arrived. No, she couldn't waste this opportunity. She had to time it just right.

When Atticus stepped onto the deck for some fresh air, Skye saw the chance. She excused herself and followed him. It was now or never.

"Thank you again for joining us, Skye," he said, looking out over the ocean. "There's something about this area that brings a lot of peace."

"I think so too. Thank you for inviting me." Skye stood beside him, also staring at the water in the distance. "Mr. Winthrop, can I ask you a question?"

"Of course."

"Is Briar my son?" The question hung out there, filled with electricity as it hovered in the air a moment, threatening to strike anyone at any minute.

Finally, Atticus chuckled. "You've got guts. I'll give you that. Why in the world would you think Briar is your child?"

"He's the right age. The right look. The right circumstance."

Atticus turned toward her, pity in his gaze. "Skye, I'm sorry if you've gotten your hopes up, but Briar isn't yours. Besides, you had a closed adoption. In order to find him, you need to hire a lawyer. Maybe—just maybe—you can find him that way."

Skye wasn't going to fall for his story. She was no longer the naïve girl who'd been desperate to belong. "I think Emma adopted my baby. That your family planned all of it from the moment I found out I was pregnant."

Atticus turned to her, something unreadable in his gaze. "I know what this is about."

Skye's back straightened as she prepared for whatever he had to say. "And what's that?"

"You want more money."

"More money?" The breath left her lungs.

"My wife told me you extorted money from her and left town."

Skye gaped at the lies that were being spewed. "That's not what happened."

"I can't give you more money, Skye I want to start this election with clean hands."

"I did not extort money." Her words came out through clenched teeth, and every ounce of her self-control had to kick into gear before she lost it. "Your wife paid me off. On her own. I had nothing to do with it."

Atticus's gaze darkened, and the friendly man present only moments ago disappeared. "Now you're insulting my family?"

"I'm telling the truth."

He turned toward her and looked her dead in the eye. "Let's just be straight with each other, Skye. You're a nice girl. But you're never going to make anything of yourself. You couldn't even afford to pay for a child. You know it's true. We both do."

Tears rushed to her eyes. He'd known how to hit her where it hurt. "I could have made it work."

"Skye, your child is better off without you." His words held authority. Definite authority.

She wiped the moisture beneath her cheeks as the words battered her.

"That's not true." Skye's voice trembled, giving away the doubt she wanted to conceal.

"This conversation is over, Skye. I'm sorry. I thought we could have a pleasant dialogue here, but I can see that's not the case. I'll let you walk yourself out. And if you come near Briar again, I'll file a restraining order against you."

CHAPTER TWENTY-ONE

TEARS MASKED Skye's vision as she hurried back inside, grabbed her purse, and rushed toward the front door. Before she could exit, someone called her name.

"Thanks for coming, Ms. Skye."

She froze before wiping her eyes and slowly turning. Briar stood there.

Her heart felt like it might burst inside her—with both love and anxiety.

Skye felt even surer than ever that this child was hers. But she'd never be able to battle such a powerful family. They'd stop her at every turn. Make her look like the bad guy. In fact, Skye would probably end up in prison or destitute if she continued to push that.

Yet how could she walk away from her child? She knew the answer.

She couldn't.

Skye leaned toward Briar, pulling herself together. "Thank you for having me today. It was really fun. And you're a really great boy."

"Sand soccer?"

She frowned. "I wish I could, but I have to go."

"Maybe another time?"

"Maybe." But Skye's heart ached again because she knew there would be a lot of obstacles before there was a next time.

Someone stepped from behind her and took her arm. "I'm here to escort you out."

She turned and saw a member of the family's security team.

"I don't need to be escorted." Skye jerked out of the man's grasp, but he reached for her again.

"The family says otherwise."

"You're squeezing my arm too hard and hurting me." She tried to get away but couldn't.

"I'll let go—as soon as you're outside."

"Don't hurt her!" Briar's face morphed with outrage. "Let her go!"

The security guard ignored him.

Everything seemed to blur around Skye as the guard pulled her to the door, as Briar protested, as more tears tried to fall.

"Hey!" a new voice said. "Get your hands off her."

Ian rushed toward them, grabbed the security guard, and jerked him back. "You're taking things too far."

The guard let go and raised his hands in the air. "I'm just doing what I was told to do."

"I'll take it from here. Briar, give me a minute, okay?"

The little boy looked at them with wide, orb-like eyes but finally nodded. "Bye, Ms. Skye."

"Bye, Briar." Part of Skye felt like she was saying goodbye forever. But she would fight to make sure that wasn't the case.

"Are you okay?" Ian asked once everyone else cleared the space.

Skye nodded, even though no part of her felt okay. "I guess so."

"I know my family is rough." His voice dipped with compassion. "I'm sorry."

"I don't fit in here. I never did." She wasn't disappointed at the realization. No, she just needed Ian to understand that and to get that look out of his eyes—the look that seemed to want more than friendship.

"You know I don't care what my family thinks."

"You never did, did you?" No, Ian was his own person. But it wasn't because he wanted to be an individual. No, it was because he was rebellious.

After a moment of silence, Ian nodded toward the door. "You want me to drive you home, Skye?"

She shook her head. "No, I have a friend picking me up."

Some of the light disappeared from Ian's gaze. "Your boyfriend?"

"He's not my boyfriend." As Austin's face flashed in her mind, the hollowness in her gut grew. Skye wished he *could* be her boyfriend. She wished those moments of bliss they'd had together could last forever. But reality could be a stronger, more formidable force than all of her wishes and dreams combined.

"Yeah, well, I'm not sure he knows that."

She turned away, her emotions bubbling to the surface too easily. "I should go. By the way, thanks for leaving that money at my produce stand."

Ian stared at her.

"The two one-hundred-dollar bills," she reminded him.

Finally he nodded. "Oh, that. You're welcome. No big deal."

"It's a big deal to me." Maybe he *had* changed.

"I hope to see you again while we're here, Skye. I don't care what my family says."

"It's probably not a good idea." Why did her soul feel like it was being ripped in two?

Ian touched her waist. "I've always thought we were a good idea, Skye."

Before his voice could roll over her anymore, she pulled the door open and stepped outside.

She had to get herself together . . . and then figure out the next step.

Austin stepped out of his truck as he saw Skye exit the house. He squinted. She didn't look happy. What exactly had happened in there?

She barely stopped long enough to look at him. No, she hurried past and climbed into his truck.

He clambered back in also and glanced at her.

She'd obviously been crying. Her cheeks and eyes were red and moist. Her actions seemed hollow and empty.

"Skye . . . ?"

She squeezed the skin between her eyes. "I need to get out of here, Austin."

"I can do that. Where do you want to go?"

She shrugged. "I don't know. I don't care. How about your place?"

Austin put the truck into drive and quietly started down the road. He wanted to demand answers. But he knew pushing that hard wasn't the way to go with Skye. She'd open up in her own time.

But his heart felt as if it was breaking a little as he watched her suffer in silence beside him.

"I'm here if you want to talk," he finally said.

"I know. Thank you." Skye still didn't make eye contact with him. No, her head was lowered, her body tense, and her face wet.

Anger burned inside him. What had they done to her? He knew going into their house was a bad idea.

His phone buzzed. As he pulled up to a stop sign, he glanced down at it. It was that stupid security system again, letting him know that his door had opened. He had to uninstall the alarm, but he hadn't had time to yet.

He pulled up to his place five minutes later and held Skye's arm as they walked up the steps.

Just as he thought, his front door was closed and locked. With Skye waiting on the porch, he checked out the rest of the place. It was clear.

After he and Skye stepped inside, Austin turned toward her. "Do you want to talk?"

She sniffed and looked away, her arms still drawn and her disposition signaling defeat. "They said that Briar isn't my son and that wherever my son is, he's better off without me. That I'm basically a walking disaster with no future."

A small sob escaped. They'd gotten into her head. They'd spoken lies as if it was the truth until Skye's confidence had become battered and bruised. Words could be such a powerful weapon.

"Oh, Skye." Austin pulled her into his arms. "You know that's not true, right?"

"No, actually, I don't. What if they're right? What if I am worthless?"

He stroked her back. "Skye, that's not true. You've got to know that."

She shook her head, stiff in his arms. "But I don't. I've got a track record to prove what they said is accurate. I can deny it all I want, but maybe they really were doing me a favor."

Austin pulled back so he could look her in the eye. "Skye, listen to me. People like the Winthrops determine a person's importance by their wealth. We know that's not true. There are far more important things in life than the numbers in a person's checking account."

"I dropped out of high school. I took drugs. I got pregnant and gave up my baby. It sounds like I've gotten all the important things wrong."

"Skye . . ." Austin had to get through to her. "I know you give away your produce to families in this area who need help. I know you put out water and food for some of the stray dogs at the campground. When I got the flu last winter, you sat with me for three days to make sure I was okay. Those are the things that show who you really are. We've all made mistakes in our past."

"Even you?"

"Even me. I've held onto bitterness and resentment. I've blamed my problems on other people. I've struggled with forgiveness. I've done stupid stuff, Skye. And I'm so glad I can be a new person through Christ. That I can put those old parts of me behind me. Sure, they're still a part of me, but they don't define me. Your past doesn't have to define you either."

Skye finally made eye contact with him, maybe a sliver of hope there in her eyes. But before she could say anything, a crack sounded outside.

Austin jerked his head toward the window just in time to see a figure standing there.

As soon as their eyes met, the man—clothed from head to toe in black—took off in a run.

"Skye, stay here," Austin said. "Lock the doors."

She nodded, almost as if she was unable to argue.

Then Austin went out the door, ready to get some answers once and for all.

~

Please, Lord, watch over him. Protect him. End this insanity.

Skye paced the floor, unable to stop thinking about what might be going on out there.

Disasters.

They did follow her everywhere.

She wanted to believe Austin's words, but she wasn't ready to yet. No, the bad in her life had definitely outweighed the good.

As much as she wanted to be with Austin, she would only ruin his life also. She was better off alone. She'd thought Lantern Beach was the place for her, but maybe she should move on. Go somewhere new. Put up more walls and not get close to anyone.

Then again, maybe what Austin said was right. She was a new person in Christ. For the first time in her life, she'd had hope these past few months. But lately, it seemed as if she'd forgotten all of that. Her emotions had consumed her life.

She had to do better. Not only for herself. But for Briar.

She couldn't let herself spiral into self-loathing. Self-doubt. Insecurity.

No, Briar needed her to be strong. Austin needed her to be strong.

And, by God's grace, Skye could do it. She could pull

herself together and be the person she needed to be in this situation.

That was what always got her in trouble—her tendency to fall back on emotion, on the easy way, on a whim. Instead, Skye was going to rely on the truth. On doing things the hard—but right—way.

As she heard a creak behind her, she started to turn.

Before she could, a gloved hand covered her mouth.

CHAPTER TWENTY-TWO

AUSTIN KEPT the man in his sights as he pushed through the maritime forest around him. The area was thick with shrubby, short plants and trees. Between the trees, vats of swamp water collected in the lowest lying areas. Mosquitoes swarmed around him, even though it was October.

But that man in black seemed to know exactly what he was doing and where he was going.

What *had* the man been doing? Spying on them? Had he been about to carry out some devious plan?

Austin continued to push forward, careful not to trip on the thick underbrush and roots.

The man he chased dodged around another tree. Where was he going? There was nothing on the other side of this brush . . . nothing but—water?

Was he headed toward the sound?

Austin didn't like this. With every new revelation and action against Skye, the feeling in his gut cinched tighter and tighter. Someone wasn't going to stop until they got what they wanted.

Finally, the trees cleared ahead.

Austin pushed himself with one last burst of energy.

But just as he reached the water, he saw the man jump into a boat. The motor roared to life, and the man raced away.

Austin stopped and caught his breath a moment as he watched the figure disappear from sight.

Who was that man?

He'd have to figure that out later. For now, he had to go check on Skye.

"You need to stay out of things," the voice behind her growled. "I tried to warn you."

Whose voice was that? Skye wasn't sure. She wasn't even sure if it sounded familiar or not.

She only knew her entire body was tense with fear. What was this man going to do to her? How had he gotten inside? Would Austin get back here in time?

The man propelled her toward the table and forced

her into a chair. "Take that pen and paper. And listen carefully. I need you to write these words."

She wanted to argue. To ask questions. But his hand remained over her mouth, pressing so hard her teeth hurt.

Skye did as he said, picking up paper and pen, knowing she had no choice. But she had no idea where he was going with this.

"Write these words: 'I'm a screwup. Nothing's ever going to change. You're all better off without me.'"

Wait . . . was he . . .?

She realized exactly what he was doing—and she couldn't go along with his plan. No way.

Something hard pressed into her head. "Do it or I'll kill your little boyfriend."

Austin? He was going to kill Austin?

"He'll come back in here, and I'll pull the trigger," the man continued. "Write the note, and I won't. Understand?"

Tears rushed to Skye's eyes. Again. Would they ever stop coming?

"Write it! 'I'm a screwup. Nothing's ever going to change. You're all better off without me.'"

Skye's hands trembled as she gripped the pen. Carefully, she wrote the words, and then braced herself for whatever would happen next.

When Skye put the pen down, the man thrust something else into her hands. "Take these."

She stared at the bottle of pain relievers.

He wanted her to overdose? And make it look a suicide?

Skye's heart rate surged. No! She couldn't do this.

Then she pictured the man shooting Austin. She couldn't let that happen either. She . . . she loved him too much.

"Take them!" the man growled.

Skye's hands shook so badly that she could hardly open the bottle. But she did. And six pills stared back.

Maybe she could throw them across the room. Buy some time.

But would that mean Austin would come back and the man would just shoot him?

"Put them in your mouth," the man ordered. "If you scream, you know what will happen."

Lord, forgive me.

Skye poured the pills into her hand. Stared at them. And with one more prayer, she put her hand to her mouth and threw her head back.

"Don't try to trick me. Swallow them."

Her throat burned. She nearly choked. She gagged.

But she swallowed the pills.

Now everyone would think she took her own life.

"Open your mouth."

The man grabbed her face and squeezed until Skye did as he asked. He checked for any hidden pills. There were none.

"Good girl," the man said.

Skye tried to steal a glance at the man. All she saw was a black mask.

Was it Ian? She didn't think so. Atticus? She doubted it. A member of their security? Most likely.

"Give it a few minutes to take effect," he said. "I hope this won't be too painful for you. This will probably be better for everyone if you're gone. At least, that's what I hear."

His words rang in her head. Better for everyone if she was gone? There were times Skye had thought that herself. What if he was right? What if she did die? No one's life would really change. It would be like she didn't matter . . . because part of her felt like she didn't.

Her head started to spin.

The pills. They were taking effect already.

Her mind wobbled. Austin's face. Briar's.

No.

This man was filling her with more lies. She did have something to live for. And her importance didn't come from anything she did or didn't do. It came from being a child of God.

The room swayed around her again.

"Good, everything is working according to plan. Now I need to leave before your boyfriend gets back. Try not to fight it. It will be easier if you don't. Good night, Skye. I hope you were a good girl. You'll find out soon where you'll be spending eternity."

Lord, help me.

Then everything went black.

CHAPTER TWENTY-THREE

AUSTIN GRUMBLED as he tromped back toward his house. He hadn't caught whoever was outside. Just what was that guy up to?

He climbed back onto his porch and knocked. "Skye. It's me. Open up."

He heard nothing.

Weird. Maybe she hadn't heard him.

He knocked again. "Skye, it's me. Austin."

Still nothing.

A bad feeling nudged his gut.

No, Skye was probably hiding. Maybe scared. Why else wouldn't she answer the door?

Answers he didn't want to consider tried to get his attention. But he wouldn't go there. Not yet.

He knocked one more time. Still nothing.

He moved to the window and cupped his hands around his eyes to see through the glare of the glass.

The first window showed his living area with his couch, chair, and TV. Nothing out of the ordinary.

He moved to the other side of the door and peered inside the window there at the kitchen.

He squinted.

Were those feet on the floor?

His heart rate surged.

Skye. Was that Skye?

He rushed to the door and shoved his shoulder against it. It took three more times until the wood splintered, and the door flew open.

He darted inside.

Skye lay on the floor. Unconscious. An empty pill bottle beside her.

"No, no, no. Skye, come back."

He put his hand to her neck. Her heart was still beating.

He grabbed his phone and called 911. As he did, his eyes fell on a paper on the kitchen table.

I'm a screwup. Nothing's ever going to change. You're all better off without me.

Had Skye done this to herself?

Had she overdosed?

No, Skye wouldn't do something like that.

She wouldn't. Austin knew her better than that.

Lord, help her. Please don't let it end this way.

Austin looked up as Ty and Cassidy came down the hallway toward him at the clinic.

Doc Clemson had pulled up some chairs across from the door to Skye's room to give Austin some privacy. He supposed there were some perks to being friends with the town's doctor.

Still, the sound of beeping hospital machines and the smell of rubbing alcohol always made Austin's blood pressure climb. Life or death could hang in the balance here, and it was a realization that wasn't lost on Austin.

Ty sat beside him and placed a hand on his back while Cassidy sat on the other side of him. He appreciated his friends coming. *No one stands alone.* That's what they'd talked about at Bible study last week, and his friends were living it.

"How is everything?" Ty asked, dropping a bag of chocolate covered raisins beside him.

"Yes, any updates?" Cassidy peered at him from the other side.

Austin shook his head, grateful that his friends were here. "No. Nothing. Not yet. Doc Clemson is in there with her. They pumped her stomach. I think she'll be okay, but . . ."

He'd thought he might lose her. Again. The thought made his insides tear apart.

Cassidy shifted beside him and lowered her voice. "Where did she get those pills?"

"To my knowledge, Skye didn't take any medications. You know Skye. As much as possible, she likes to keep things all natural. She hesitated to even take Tylenol."

"Austin, I went into her camper . . ." Cassidy licked her lips.

He twisted his head, not understanding where Cassidy was going with this. "Okay . . ."

"After you guys saw the intruder there, I checked everything out. She had bottles of prescription pain killers in one of her drawers."

Austin shook his head, not buying it. "If Skye had them there, it's because the intruder planted them. I'm telling you, she hates taking any kind of drug. Was her name on the bottles?"

"No, the labels had been pulled off."

"Just like at my house. There was no name on that bottle either."

"I saw the note, Austin," Cassidy said, her voice still low. "Was that her handwriting?"

Austin's throat burned. He didn't want to answer the

question. But Cassidy was waiting. And he couldn't avoid her forever.

Finally, he nodded. "Yeah, it looked like her handwriting."

"You think she wrote it under duress?" Ty leaned forward, his elbows on his knees.

Austin shrugged, his head pounding. "I don't know what to think. I know she's taking everything really hard—the fact that she gave up her son for adoption. That the Winthrops may have manipulated her into doing it so their daughter could have the child she'd always wanted. Skye feels a lot of guilt and shame."

Cassidy frowned, and Austin wasn't sure if she was in cop mode or friend mode. Most likely, both. But he didn't like these questions.

"That's what I thought," she finally said. "She's having trouble forgiving herself."

"Exactly. But I don't think she would have tried to end it all. She wanted to know if Briar was hers. She wanted answers. Justice." He knew Skye better than this. She was a fighter.

"I don't think Skye did this to herself either," Cassidy said.

Relief filled Austin. Good. Someone else believed in her.

"We're going to find out what happened," Ty added.

Cassidy nodded. "Until then, could you go over everything one more time?"

Austin told them about the noise outside. The figure fleeing through the woods. How he'd chased him.

Had that just been a distraction? Had this person's goal all along been to draw Austin out so they could enact this part of their plan?

"So you're thinking there are two people involved?" Cassidy said.

Austin nodded. "I know I followed that man for as long as I could. He didn't have time to do this after I finished chasing him. There are two people involved here."

"I tried to talk to the Winthrops this morning," Cassidy said. "They weren't home, but the security team and maid said the family was all home last night."

"Convenient."

"I know. However, at this point, there's nothing to prove they're behind this or trying to run her off the road or even your scaffolding accident. But I'm not giving up on that lead. These people have money and resources."

"Skye had lunch with them today," Austin said. "She looked pretty upset afterward. They were rough on her, and I don't trust them."

"We'll get to the bottom of this." Cassidy laid a hand on his arm and leveled her voice. "I have to say that whoever is behind this is clever. Each of these incidents could be written off as accidents or as self-inflicted. Sometimes, these are the worst kind of people to deal with."

Austin's stomach clenched. He agreed with Cassidy's assessment—he just didn't like it.

At that moment, a figure appeared at the end of the hallway.

Austin stood. It was Ian.

CHAPTER TWENTY-FOUR

WHY IN THE world would that man show his face here?

"Austin, don't do anything foolish," Ty said, standing beside him.

Austin couldn't promise that.

"You have a lot of nerve showing up here." Austin stopped Ian before he reached Skye's door.

Ian raised his hands in the air and took a step back. "I'm not here to start trouble."

"Then why are you here?"

"I heard what happened, and I came to check on Skye."

"How'd you hear?" Cassidy asked. "This hasn't been made public in any way."

"I know, I know. But my sister cut herself on a broken

shell while walking on the beach. We were in the waiting room, and I thought I heard Skye's name."

Waiting room? Cut herself?

What if it hadn't been a broken shell that had caused her injury?

Could his sister have been the person Austin chased?

Austin couldn't say for sure. He hadn't gotten a good look at the man outside his house, and he'd just assumed it had been a man he chased. But the figure was thin and lithe. Could it have been a woman?

Even more so—could it have been Ian's sister?

"Is Skye okay?" Ian asked. "Despite our history, I still consider her a friend."

"I heard." Austin tried to keep the bitterness out of his words. If he'd been Ian, he would have never let his parents treat Skye that way. He would have stood up for her.

"So?"

"She's recovering." Austin's jaw tensed as he said the words. "That's all I know."

An irritated puff of air escaped from Ian. "You can't tell me what happened?"

"Nope."

Ian's expression morphed from concerned to . . . what was that? Manipulative? Mischievous?

"She's always been a handful," he finally said, his eyes sparkling.

The man was trying to start trouble, Austin realized.

His jaw clenched tighter. "What do you mean?"

"She told you about going to prison, didn't she?" The sparkle reached Ian's voice, and a trace of satisfaction lifted his words.

Austin tried not to flinch, tried not to play Ian's game. The man was just trying to put ideas into his head. "What are you talking about? Skye's never been to prison. She went to jail once for stealing her boyfriend's drugs, if that's what you're talking about."

The start of a smile curled Ian's lip. "Oh, I didn't mean jail. I meant prison. She got desperate and stole some money. I couldn't really blame her. I mean, she had a hard life and wasn't raised with many morals."

Ty nudged him, as if he sensed Austin's rising anger as well as his desire to punch this guy in his smug little face.

"Some people were raised with everything, and they still act like complete jerks," Austin snapped.

Ian's eyebrows flickered up. "Touché. Point taken. I'm just saying, Skye does what she has to do to get what she wants. Don't let her fool you."

"Yeah, you sound like a great friend," Ty said. "I mean, friends should do everything in their power to make their friend sound desperate and to paint them in the worst light possible."

Ian's gaze darkened. "I'm just telling you the truth. I've always loved Skye—even when she's screwed up. The question is: Can you?"

Austin fisted his hands again. But at just that moment, the door behind him opened. Doc Clemson stepped out, and his eyes connected with Austin's.

"She's okay," he said.

The air left his lungs. Thank goodness, Austin had found her before it was too late.

"And she wants to see you," the doctor continued.

Skye braced herself to see Austin.

What did he think of her right now? Did he believe Skye had actually done this? If so, she wasn't sure her heart could handle it.

She tried to smile when Austin stepped inside, but Skye wasn't sure if the action actually reached her lips or not. Seeing Austin made her heart swell . . . with both love and angst.

The two of them had come so close—so close to maybe giving a relationship a shot.

And then the truth came out, and everything was ruined. Her stomach clenched at the memories.

Austin sat in a chair beside her and squeezed her hand. "How are you?"

"I've been better." She licked her lips, knowing she looked like death in the hospital gown. "That man made me write that note."

"I knew you didn't write it, that someone had forced you. Did you recognize him?"

"I couldn't see his face. He wore a mask, but I think the other man was meant to be a distraction. This guy must have been hiding in the closet or something. As soon as you left, he jumped into action." She flinched as the memories hit her.

"Did you recognize his voice?"

Skye shook her head. She'd replayed it so many times in her mind, but she still had no answers. "No, I didn't. I really have no idea who he is. But if you hadn't found me when you did . . ."

Austin squeezed her hand, the expression on his face clearly showing that he'd been afraid of losing her. "Everything is going to be okay, Skye."

"Nothing feels okay." Her voice cracked as she said the words. She was fighting against something—someone —formidable. Yet she couldn't seem to give up.

"I'll make sure everything is okay. I promise you."

Austin's words almost made Skye believe him. But things didn't work out okay in her life. They never had. And she had no hope they ever would.

She hated that the thoughts had even crossed her mind. But they were there because she believed them. They'd become her truth, no matter what she tried to tell herself.

A knock sounded at the door, pulling them from their conversation.

Cassidy stepped inside, a sympathetic look on her face. "I'm going to need to ask you a few questions."

Skye nodded, ready to repeat her story . . . again.

CHAPTER TWENTY-FIVE

"YOU HAVEN'T RUN AWAY YET," Skye muttered as Austin stepped into her room the next morning.

He came to stand at her bedside. "Why would I run away?"

She could think of a million reasons. But she didn't bring them up now. Instead, she reveled in the fact he was here. And she reminded herself that there were still things she needed to tell him. And she would. In good time.

Cassidy had already been by and brought Skye some clean clothes. She'd taken a shower and cleaned herself up so she felt halfway human. It was a small thing, but it made her feel ten times better.

She squinted, studying Austin for a minute. His hair still looked rumpled, and his gaze showed he was tired.

"You look worse than I do," she told him.

That was when it hit her.

"You slept in the hallway all night, didn't you?"

Austin shrugged, not denying it. "Someone had to keep an eye on you."

"But you're still recovering from your fall," she said, knowing the argument was useless.

"You're more important."

Warmth spread through her. He meant the words. Skye knew he did.

"When are you being discharged?" Austin asked.

"Any time." Right on cue, Doc Clemson came in with the paperwork. Skye signed off, and Austin took her hand as she slid off the bed, ready to go.

"Let's get out of here." Austin squeezed her hand.

A moment later, they were in his truck. Jitters rumbled through Skye. It could be because of the overdose . . . or because she was around Austin. It was a toss-up. But she had some revelations last night, some things that only almost losing her life could produce.

"Could we stop by the ocean?" she asked.

"Sure. If that's what you want."

"I can always think more clearly at the ocean."

"Yeah, I get that." He pulled off at one of the public beach-access points. As they climbed from his truck, Austin took her hand into his.

Skye knew she should probably pull away. But she couldn't. When she was with Austin, she felt like everything would be okay. Like she could conquer the world.

That added boost was what she needed to get through this.

She was selfish to take his hand, yet she felt powerless to say no to the very thing she craved.

They went to the base of one of the dunes and sat there. The waves still looked gray and angry today, but there were a few people who'd ventured into their depths anyway.

"It's a shame when other people have to put their lives on the line to save one of these guys who ignore the red flags," Austin said.

"Yeah, it is." Was that what Skye was doing? Putting Austin's life on the line because she was ignoring the signs of danger? Guilt nipped at her again.

"Why do you hate water so much, Skye?" Austin asked. "You never told me."

She stared out into the tempest. "I told you earlier that Ian and I did some stupid things when we dated. But the dumbest thing we did was stealing a yacht."

"You stole a yacht?" Surprise lilted his voice.

Skye nodded as memories tried to pummel her again. With the memories came shame and regret—shame and regret that she needed to let go of. "Well, Ian stole the yacht, but I went along for the ride."

"But Ian is wealthy. Didn't his family have their own boat?"

And that was the irony of it all.

"They did, but it wasn't enough to enjoy the things freely given to him. He needed to push the limits. Ian got some kind of high from it."

"Sounds unhealthy, to say the least."

"When we got caught by the marine police, he pushed me into the water so we could both escape. He jumped in after me and began swimming away. I don't think he realized I couldn't swim." Her voice caught. "Or maybe he did. But I almost drowned in the ocean. I tried to doggy paddle, to grab the side of the boat, to do whatever I could. But it didn't matter. I just kept sinking and couldn't keep my head above water. I've never felt so helpless."

"That's why you hate water . . ." Dull understanding spread through his voice.

She nodded. "Exactly. Law officials rescued me, and Ian's parents paid off the yacht owner so he wouldn't press charges. That was when things started to get rocky between Ian and me. It was the beginning of the end. Except I realized a few days later that I was pregnant."

Silence stretched a moment, and she gave Austin space to process what she'd just told him.

"Is it true that you went to prison, Skye?" Austin finally asked, picking up a broken piece of dune grass and twisting it in his fingers. "I mean, you told me about the time you were arrested for breaking into a boyfriend's house and stealing drugs. But . . ."

She sucked in a breath. He knew. But how? It didn't really matter because the truth was the truth, no matter how he found out.

"I'm not judging you, Skye," Austin prodded. "I'm just trying to peel back the layers."

Skye ran her hand through the soft, grainy sand as her past hit her full force. "Not long after the baby was born— probably a year later—I began working as a receptionist for a financial planning company. Somehow, money was siphoned into my account from one of the client's."

"What?" His voice punched with disbelief.

Skye nodded grimly, knowing if she stopped now, she might not ever finish. "I didn't do it. I wouldn't have any idea how to do it, but the police didn't believe that. I went to prison for three years. I couldn't prove my innocence. When I got out, I just wanted a new life in a new place. I moved here, and I changed my last name to my mother's maiden name so I could leave my past behind. Until my past showed up here."

Austin took her hand and softly kissed it. "Thanks for sharing that, Skye."

"Yeah, it's overdue. I'm sorry. I didn't want to disappoint you. I know I keep saying that. It's just that I wouldn't blame you if you did—"

"You didn't disappoint, Skye. But how about if neither of us keep secrets anymore."

"I'd like that." He was right—in a way, it was such a relief to put everything out there. She hadn't realized how heavy the burden of silence was or how refreshing total honesty could feel.

As much as she wanted to sit here all day with Austin, she knew that couldn't happen.

Instead, she glanced at her watch. "And I hate to change the subject, but you have a kayaking trip you need to do."

"I can't leave you."

"I've already arranged things with Cassidy," she said. "I'm going to stay with her today. I'll ride along or sit at the police station or do whatever I have to do. But I'll be careful."

"Skye . . ."

"You promised Wes you'd help, and I know he's counting on it. Don't let me hold you back."

Based on his frown, Austin wasn't happy to be leaving her. But Skye hadn't left him much choice. She'd covered her bases.

Besides, she really wanted to talk to Cassidy about her next plan of action. She knew Austin wouldn't approve. But if Skye was going to put this to rest, she was going to have to take desperate measures.

"How are you feeling?" Cassidy asked as she and Skye cruised down the road an hour later.

Skye stared out the window. The wind tossed tree branches back and forth as more turbulent weather blew into the area. "I'm okay. I'm . . . well, I guess I'm getting there, at least. My first inclination throughout all of this was to slip back into my old ways. To do whatever it took to get what I wanted. But I'm not going to do that."

Skye wasn't sure what had changed. She only knew that the events of the past few days had triggered something inside her, some kind of resolution to deal with her past head on. If she ever wanted a future with Austin, she needed closure. And it would be worth it. For Austin's sake.

No, make that for her *own* sake.

"I'm really proud of you, Skye. I know that's hard."

Skye nodded, realizing with certainty that she wasn't the same person she'd been. And every decision she made from here on out would either solidify that or undo it. She chose to solidify it.

"It wasn't easy," Skye said. "Honestly, Jimmy James offered me an easy way to make some of the money I would need to pay the legal bills. I was tempted for a moment. But I'm not going to do that, Cassidy. I'm going to do things the right way."

"I'm not even going to ask right now what kind of offer Jimmy James made you. That's a conversation for a different day." Cassidy did a half eye roll when she mentioned Jimmy James. "I think you'll find doing things the right way is the most satisfying way, Skye. It builds character."

Cassidy pulled to a stop in front of the Winthrops' rental and put the cruiser in park. But she made no move to climb out.

"I'm keeping an eye on them today—although I don't think they'd be stupid enough to try anything else," Cassidy explained.

"You talked to them?" Skye's breath caught. What had Cassidy found out? Anything new?

"I stopped by there this morning to chat with them. Believe me, Quinton and I have been busy. Mac even came in to help us. We dusted for fingerprints at Austin's place. We checked security cameras around the island. We also talked to members of the Winthrops' security team and even the nanny. No one apparently knows anything. And without sufficient evidence, we can't get a warrant to search their home."

"The family didn't become the powerhouse they are by being stupid," Skye said, remembering again just how insurmountable this seemed.

"I agree. We're far from being done with this case, Skye. We're going to figure out who's been behind these incidents. Unfortunately, things aren't moving quickly. But that's okay. We'll do this the right way, and the bad guy will get his justice."

"I appreciate all you're doing, Cassidy," Skye said, glancing at her friend. "And I'm grateful to have you in my life."

"Back at you, Skye. You were one of my first friends here, and I've never forgotten that. You literally gave me the coat off your back the first time we hung out. That says a lot."

Silence fell for a few minutes, and they both watched the Winthrop house. Nothing was happening. Not yet, at least.

"How about you and Austin?" Cassidy took a sip of her coffee. "Do you mind if I ask what's going on?"

Skye glanced down at her hands. Austin had really been all she'd been thinking about. She'd be a fool to let him walk away. But he'd be a fool to keep her. She wanted to let the thoughts go but couldn't.

"I love him, Cassidy. I really do. But I don't know if I'm the right one for him. He deserves someone without so much baggage."

"I'm pretty sure he would beg to differ. We all have baggage, Skye."

"Even you and Ty, the perfect couple?" Skye glanced at her friend, the one who seemed to have it all together.

Cassidy let out a quick laugh. "Yeah, even me and Ty. Relationships are about two imperfect people coming together and fighting to make things work. Personally, I think you and Austin are great together. You balance each other out."

Skye pondered her words for a moment, wondering if they just might be true.

"For a long time, I wondered if Austin was a player," Skye admitted. "He dated women but never seemed to want to settle down. A confirmed bachelor. But my opinion has been slowly changing."

"He's been in love with you since the moment I first saw the two of you together. I don't think you're a flash in the pan for him, Skye. I think when you find the right person that restlessness subsides. I think Austin is that person."

Skye brushed a hair back from her eyes, hope beginning to grow inside her. Maybe Cassidy was right. If Skye made it out of all this alive, she was going to stop hiding behind her mistakes. She was going to acknowledge that she might make more mistakes in the future, but she couldn't fear them. No, she'd learn from them.

"Thanks, Cassidy. I appreciate that."

"What are you going to do about Briar?"

Skye licked her lips. This was the part of the conversation she'd been anticipating—or dreading, depending on the moment. She'd thought long and hard about this last night, and only one solution made sense. "I think I'm going to go public."

Cassidy did a double take. "Are you sure that's a good idea?"

"No, I'm not. But I don't have other choices. I'll be threatening the thing that's most important to the family—their reputation. Maybe that's the only way I'll make any progress."

"But—"

"Before you saying anything, I want to say that I've been avoiding risks for the past few years, figuring it was safer if I didn't take any chances," Skye continued. "I'm ready to step beyond that. This is what I have to do, Cassidy."

"Then, I can respect that."

Hearing Cassidy say that made relief wash over Skye. A little support really could go a long way.

Before they could talk anymore, Cassidy's phone rang.

"Speak of the devil . . . it's Jimmy James." Cassidy put the phone to her ear. Her voice morphed from professional to intrigued. "Thanks. I'll be right there."

"What is it?" Skye held onto hope that it might have something to do with the case.

"There's an SUV that matches the description of the one that ran you off the road," Cassidy said. "It's parked down at the marina near where Jimmy James works. I asked him to keep an eye out for it."

"The Winthrops are renting a slip down there," Skye said. How could she not have thought of that? Ginger had even mentioned that Atticus and Ian were out sailing one day.

"Let's go see if there's a scrape on the side from where it hit your bike."

Skye nodded. This just might be their best lead yet.

Skye and Cassidy arrived at the marina and pulled into one of the parking spaces there. Around them, the wind had picked up, sending boats bobbing and a few pieces of trash tumbling across the asphalt.

The place was surprisingly quiet right now, especially compared to the hustle and bustle of activity here during the summer months.

Skye glanced around. Saw all the boats in their slips. Saw crab pods lined up on the edge of the property. Saw the trucks people used to pull their boats here before launching them into the water.

"There's the SUV." Skye nodded toward one in the distance.

"Let me go check it out," Cassidy said, turning professional again. "You stay here. With the doors locked. Got it?"

Skye nodded, having no desire to put herself in danger. "Got it."

Besides, she didn't have the physical energy to do anything. No, her body was still recovering after everything that had happened. Those pills she'd been forced to swallow. Having her stomach pumped. The distress of it all had taken its toll.

As Cassidy started toward the SUV, a man darted out from the other side of it and took off in a run. Cassidy sprinted after him.

Please, Lord. Watch over her. Give us answers.

Just then, a tap sounded on the glass beside her. Skye

looked up and saw someone standing there. With a gun. Pointed directly at her.

Maybe she should have been more careful what she prayed.

"Get out of the car. If you scream, I'll pull this trigger on you. And then I'll find your boyfriend and do the same."

CHAPTER TWENTY-SIX

SKYE'S GAZE came into focus as she stared out the window and her heart stuttered a few beats. "Ian?"

He narrowed his eyes, all his rich-boy charm and I'm-not-the-same-person claims gone. "Stop talking and get out. I'll shoot you. Don't test me."

Based on the crazy look in his eyes, Ian was telling the truth. Skye raised her hands and stepped from the police cruiser. Ian shoved the gun into her side. Her heart slammed into her ribcage. Just what was he planning here?

She stole a glance over her shoulder, hoping Cassidy was headed back. But she'd disappeared behind the bait-and-tackle shop.

Had Ian planned that? Just like he'd lured Austin out

of the house to chase after that man while someone else had forced Skye to overdose?

Now that she thought about it, that's what Ian had done when he'd stolen that yacht. He'd distracted the owner by saying his car was on fire, and then he'd jumped onboard.

"We've got to move before your friend gets back. Now go."

With the gun stabbing at Skye's ribs and a hard grip on her arm, Ian led her to the water.

Toward a cabin cruiser, probably twenty-four-feet long with a huge motor.

Horrible visions of what Ian might have in mind battered her thoughts. She wasn't going to walk away from this, was she?

"Get on," Ian ordered.

"Ian, you don't have to do this."

"Of course I do. Now get on."

He shoved the gun harder until Skye yelped. Her entire body trembled as she stepped onboard the boat. Ian jumped on right behind her, jerked the ropes from the dock, and dragged Skye toward the cockpit.

The boat was already running and waiting. Ian only had to hit a few things before they pulled from the marina. He'd thought of everything, hadn't he? No doubt, he'd kept that SUV out of sight, only bringing it here to draw Cassidy's attention. If he'd been watching the clinic, he would have known the two of them were together today.

Skye glanced back just in time to see Cassidy return to her police cruiser and glance around. Based on how Ian was standing next to her Cassidy probably hadn't even seen her.

Despair tried to bite into her, but Skye pushed it away.

"What are you going to do with me?" she finally asked.

Ian's iron-tight grip remained on her. Skye was tempted to fight back—but there was nowhere to go. And he still had a gun in one hand. She had no doubt he would use it.

"I'm going to keep you quiet, once and for all. I should have sealed this deal a long time ago."

Nausea gurgled in her gut. But she couldn't give in to despair. No, she'd done that for too long. She had to keep a cool head here.

"You've been behind this the whole time?" The wind slapped her in the face and made her hair feel like whips as the strands hit her cheeks. They left the no-wake zone, and Ian accelerated toward the open horizon in the distance. Anxiety surged up her spine.

"I tried to give subtle hints for you to stay away, but it

didn't work. I wasn't sure what my next plan of action was. Luckily, this came together just in time."

"Why would you do this, Ian?" Skye knew he was self-absorbed and wild. But a killer? Someone who knowingly hurt people? Skye didn't want to believe it. Yet Ian was leaving her no other choice.

"Because you're going to ruin everything for me. I've been working for the past two years on cleaning up my reputation. I can't have you come in and undo all of my work."

Skye glanced around again, looking for anything that might help her out. But there was nothing. And every time she thought about trying to physically take Ian, she felt the gun in her side.

Was her only hope that her friends would find her? But Austin was kayaking with Wes. Cassidy hadn't seen her leave. By the time anyone figured out what happened, it would be too late.

"You don't care about reputation," she said, raising her voice to be heard over the roar of the boat's engine. "You never have."

"That's where you're wrong. I do care. I have to care if I want to take over my father's business."

Her breath caught. "What are you talking about?"

"My father thinks it's important that if our company is going to maintain its wholesome image that I clean up my act. If you interfere, all of my hard work is going to be for nothing."

"How am I interfering?" She wasn't the one who'd sought him out. All she'd done was ask questions and put facts together.

"Because you discovered Briar."

Her heart skipped a beat as the truth rang out loud and clear. "He's our son, isn't he?"

Ian's eyes narrowed, as if annoyed. "I guess I can tell you now since you won't live to tell anyone else about it. So, yes, he is. He's a nice blend of the two of us, isn't he?"

"Does he know you're his father?" Skye just couldn't figure out what Ian was thinking—only that he wasn't in his right mind. And that scared her more than anything because he had a goal in mind right now.

"Are you kidding me?" He let out a gruff chuckle. "No way. The last thing I need is some kid looking up to me."

This man disgusted Skye in so many ways. How could she have honestly thought he'd changed? "How is killing me going to help anything?"

"You won't be alive to ruin my life, for starters. If you come forward with the truth about what my family did to you, my reformed image will be gone. Not only that, my father will probably lose the election and won't want to hand over the reins of his company."

"Why do you want to run the company so badly? I didn't think that was your thing."

"Let's just say my trust fund ran out, and my dad isn't budging. He said I have to earn my keep."

"And you can't bear the thought of giving up your extravagant lifestyle, can you?" At one time, Skye had thought it might be nice to have that luxury. Now it was sounding more like a curse.

"Why would I ever want to do that? I have a good life."

Skye gritted her teeth, still aware of the gun at her side. "You've got to be the most selfish person I've ever met."

"Well, you're the one who fell in love with me."

If only she hadn't, but since she couldn't erase the past, she was going to have to learn from it. "How are you going to kill me? You going to try and overdose me again?"

"No, but that was a brilliant move now, wasn't it? You were in a bad place emotionally. No one would suspect that I forced you to take those pills. The problem was that your boyfriend came back too quickly and your will to live was too strong."

"And you tried to run me off the road?"

"Again, it could have looked like an accident." He stared out over the water, not even flinching at what he'd done.

"You even tampered with Austin's construction site. Why would you do that?"

"I thought if he was hurt that might distract you from being nosy. I know how you are. I knew as soon as you saw Briar that you'd get suspicious. The art of diversion is one of the best."

"Is it?"

"It is. Is one of your company's products failing? Causing lawsuits because of rashes and other conditions? Bury that story by donating to charity, by releasing a new product, by schmoozing the press. It's pretty amazing, actually."

"But someone saw your sister at the job site." What sense did that make?

"I told her she should go check it out, that it was a good piece of investment property and that the owners were putting in up for sale soon. I figured her presence would throw the police off long enough to buy me time." His voice rang with smug satisfaction.

"You set up your own sister." Skye's throat burned with realization. He really was ruthless. "I suppose you're the one who messed with the security system at Austin's house?"

He smiled again, looking entirely too satisfied. "I had one of my guys do it for me. We didn't actually know your little boyfriend had a security system, but when we discovered it, we decided to use it to our advantage. I thought planting the pain killers at your house was a nice touch also. I didn't know how I could use it to my advantage, but I figured there was a way, especially with your history. And I was right."

Anger burned inside her. "If only you could put this much energy into making money, maybe you'd stand a chance."

"Well, I've done everything I could to get you out of my life and it didn't work."

She fisted her hands. "What does that mean?"

"It means I convinced my mom to give you that money. I . . ." His voice trailed.

"You set me up at my job, didn't you? You planted that evidence that had me arrested."

The wind slapping her face was the only thing cooling her off.

"Well, I didn't do it myself, but I had someone help me. I really just wanted to get rid of you because I thought you would figure out things eventually, and I was right."

He slowed the boat as they reached the churning Atlantic Ocean. Skye glanced around. Nothing but water surrounded them.

Skye's head spun as fear whipped through her.

"You know what's coming next, don't you?" Ian smiled, almost like he was enjoying this.

"Don't do this, Ian," Skye said.

"I'm sorry, but you left me no choice." He stopped the boat and grabbed her arm.

"You always have a choice. You won't get away with this." The boat bobbed, nearly knocking her off-balance. She'd never had sea legs.

"I think I will. Now move to the edge of the boat and let's get this over with. According to some of the fisherman I overheard, the sharks are really biting lately. You're in for a fun time, one way or another."

Just as Austin pulled the last kayak back to the sandy shore bordering the sound, his phone rang. He straightened, took a step away from the rest of the group, and glanced at the screen.

They'd just gotten back, and the group had been a handful. What Austin really wanted was to see Skye and spend the rest of the day with her. But Wes had needed his help today.

In fact, one of the women hadn't listened to directions and had been sucked into a current that pulled her out toward the ocean. Austin had reached her kayak just in time.

Cassidy's name appeared on his screen. Anxiety

snaked up his spine as he put the phone to his ear. Cassidy never called—unless something was wrong.

"Skye is gone," she announced.

Adrenaline pumped through Austin's blood, and he froze. "What do you mean she's gone?"

"I left her locked in my car while I went to question someone. The questioning turned into a chase. When I got back, Skye was gone."

Gone? How could she just be gone? "Any sign of a struggle?"

"No, none. I'm sorry, Austin. I don't know what happened, but I have people out searching for her. I wanted to let you know."

He glanced back and saw most of the bridal party that had been on the tour today were already leaving for another adventure. Wes and Colton could handle cleaning up the kayaks and putting them away. Austin had to go find Skye.

"Where are you?" Austin needed to get there. See things for himself. Search for Skye himself.

"I'm at the marina."

"I'll be right there."

As Austin hung up, he looked over and saw that, at some point, Wes had joined him.

"I don't know what happened," his friend said. "But if you're going somewhere, I'm driving you."

"You've got to clean up here."

"Colton can handle it. Let's go."

They pulled up to the marina ten minutes later. Cassidy and Ty were already there, along with Officer Quinton, the marine police, and a state police officer. Cassidy met him as soon as he got out of the car.

"No one saw anything," Cassidy said. "She was in my cruiser. I came back five minutes later, and she was gone. I did see a boat pulling away at that time, but I didn't see Skye. The Coast Guard patrol is out there now looking for it, just in case."

"That's all you know?" He needed more than that to go on.

"Right now. I'm so sorry, Austin."

"Where are the Winthrops?"

Cassidy frowned. "I don't know. Quinton is headed over to their house."

"Skye said they had a boat here. Is it still here?" The questions kept coming.

"It is. It's right over there."

Austin remembered his earlier conversation with Skye —the one where she'd told him about being left in the ocean to die—and the sick feeling in his gut grew. "Cassidy, I'm nearly certain she was on the boat that left. The security guard you chased was just a distraction."

"What?" Cassidy's eyes widened.

Austin glanced around until he spotted Jimmy James across the marina, hosing off a Bayliner. "I'm going to go talk to him."

"Austin, don't do anything rash," Cassidy warned. "I need to stay here and coordinate the efforts, so I can't go with you."

"Got it." Austin darted over toward Jimmy James, who tensed when he saw him. "I need a boat. Now."

"I don't have a boat." Jimmy James stepped away, as if taken back.

"Can you get me one?"

"Maybe." He shrugged and released his grip on the water hose. "Why?"

"Jimmy James, Skye is in trouble. I need a boat. Now."

The burly man nodded slowly as realization rolled over him. He reached into his pocket. "Okay, here's the one I was working on. Just don't mess it up or I'll get fired."

Wes was on his heels as he hopped onto the Bayliner. Austin started the engine. Before they pulled from the dock, Ty also hopped on. "You're not doing this without me."

Having a former Navy SEAL on board would only help them.

They raced out into the water, searching for a sign of any other boats.

"Any idea where they could have gone?" Ty asked.

"If I had to guess, somewhere that's most dangerous."

"That would be the ocean."

"We've got to find her. She can't swim," he reminded his friends.

"We will. Here, let me steer the boat. You keep a look-out." Ty took the wheel.

As he did, Austin searched the open expanse of water, praying above all else that she was okay.

CHAPTER TWENTY-SEVEN

"PLEASE DON'T DO THIS, IAN," Skye said, staring at the whitecaps all around her.

"Sorry, beautiful. It's the only way."

"I can be quiet." She was desperate and needed to buy time.

Ian let out a quick, short laugh. "No, you can't. When you believe in something, you push for it. Don't deny it."

"Ian . . ." Skye desperately tried to think of another tactic but couldn't. She was at Ian's mercy.

"Make this easy on me. Jump in." Ian pointed to the water with his gun.

She stared at the angry ocean, and her skin crawled. She wouldn't survive for more than five minutes out there. Even if she managed to stay afloat, the current would pull her under. She'd heard the stories.

"I'm not making anything easy on you," she finally said, stubborn determination kicking in

"Have it your way." Ian's hand hit her shoulder.

Skye toppled forward but caught herself before she flipped over the side of the boat.

"Oh, you have to be spunky," he muttered.

He put his gun down on the captain's chair, and his arms wrapped around Skye, pinning her arms against her and making her unable to move.

She stared at the gun. If only she could reach it. If she could grab it and maybe turn this situation around.

But it was no use. Ian was stronger than she was. Too strong.

Skye kicked and thrashed, but it did no good.

With a few grunts, he had her off her feet. He jerked his body, trying to get her to do what he wanted.

The next instant, Skye hung over the side of the boat. She sucked in a breath, trying not to panic.

"Ian, don't!"

Ian let go. Her feet hit the water. But her arms flailed out, and she caught the edge of the boat. A wave lapped over her, spraying water into her mouth.

But she wasn't cut loose. Not yet.

"Good try, beautiful." Ian stepped closer.

If only Skye could pull herself back in.

She glanced up at Ian again, saw him peering down at her with a glimmer in his gaze.

No, no, no . . .

She tightened her grip, but the side of the boat was wet. Her fingers slipped.

Ian smiled at her one last time before prying her fingers up. "See you on the other side, Skye. It was fun."

And then he let go.

The water consumed Skye. Buried her. Took her breath away.

Just as her head bobbed to the surface, she saw Ian's boat pulling away.

He really was leaving her out here in the middle of the ocean. And by the time anyone found her, she'd be dead.

"Over there!" Austin yelled.

He spotted two boats bobbing in the water in the distance. Could Skye be on one of them? It was a long shot, but he had to keep hope alive.

"It looks like a Coast Guard patrol boat," Ty said, pushing his sunglasses up higher. "Maybe they found Skye."

Austin's heart rate surged. Maybe this nightmare was

over. Maybe Skye was safe, and whoever was behind this had been arrested.

Please, Lord . . .

They pulled up beside the boat, and one of the Coast Guard crew members came to the edge to speak to them.

"We're looking for our friend, Skye Lavinia," Austin said above the grind of the boat engines. "We believe a man named Ian Winthrop abducted her."

Just as Austin said the words, he spotted Ian on the other side of the boat. His hands were behind his back. In handcuffs, Austin realized.

Austin's gaze darted around. Ian. Was he the one behind this? He had to be.

And if Ian was here . . . where was Skye?

Austin hopped over the edge of his boat and onto the Coast Guard vessel.

"Hey!" The coastguardsman put a hand out to stop Austin before he got near Ian.

"We just arrested that man, but the woman isn't with him," the coastguardsman said.

"Where is she?" Austin yelled, the veins at his neck throbbing.

The coastguardsman continued to restrain Austin before he could reach Ian. It was probably better that way because if Austin got his hands on Ian . . . he didn't know what he'd do. Something he'd regret, probably.

Ian just smiled back, looking entirely too smug. "I don't know what you're talking about."

"You left her out there in the ocean again, didn't you? Where?" Austin started to lunge at him again, but the coastguardsman held him back.

"We have our guys out there looking. She can't be very far. We picked him up only a few minutes ago."

"I'm not giving up," Austin said, determination making his spine rigid.

He hopped back into his boat again, and Ty took off.

They were going to find Skye. They had to.

Because Austin wasn't coming back until he did.

CHAPTER TWENTY-EIGHT

THE WATER SWALLOWED SKYE AGAIN.

If only she could touch bottom.

But she couldn't. And she wouldn't be able to—not until she got much closer to shore. But she couldn't even see the shore, so her hopes of trying to reach it were slim.

She glanced around. How deep was it out here? A hundred feet?

Probably more.

Skye couldn't think about that. If she did, panic would set in. No, she needed to try and float.

That was right.

If she could stay afloat, then she might survive until someone found her.

But her arms and legs were cold. Hypothermia might set in after a while. What was the water temperature? If she had to guess, it was sixty-some degrees out here. But it felt so cold.

Someone would find her.

The thoughts warred inside Skye as hope and despair collided.

Float, she reminded herself again.

She popped her legs up and tried to relax, to conserve her energy. Skye may not be able to swim, but she could do her best to stay above water.

Another wave washed over her, and panic tried to seize her again as her face went underwater.

She raised her head just long enough to glance around. In front of her was nothing but water.

To her left, more water.

To her right, even more water.

Which direction was land? She'd gotten turned around after Ian's boat had disappeared. And now she had no idea.

Carefully, she glanced behind her and blinked.

Was that a . . . boat?

It was far away. But . . . yes! It was a boat.

She righted herself, desperate to draw the attention of those on board. She had to wave her hands—do something so they would see her.

But as she tried to lift her arms, another wave crashed over her and filled her lungs with water.

"We've got too big of an area to cover," Austin said, his jaw throbbing as he clenched his teeth.

Ty continued to drive the boat forward, even as the wind whipped around them and choppy waves jerked their bodies in ways they weren't meant to be jerked. The small craft advisory that had just been issued was no joke.

"The Coast Guard is out here helping," Ty reminded him.

"There's a storm blowing in," Austin said. "I'm afraid we're going to be too late."

"We can't think like that." Ty glanced back at him. "We'll find her, Austin."

Austin scanned the horizon again. With waves like this, it would be hard to see anyone in the water. Their best hope was to spot the boat with Skye on it. But there was also a chance she wasn't on that boat anymore.

He didn't want to think about that.

Whenever Austin closed his eyes, he pictured himself finding Skye.

Dead.

In the water.

He shook his head. No, Ty was right. He couldn't think like that. He had to keep hope alive and stay positive.

"Austin, Ty, what's that over there?" Wes yelled, pointing in the distance.

Austin squinted. Something was in the water.

Was it buoy? A crab pod?

Or could it be a person?

Did he even dare hope . . .

"Let's go closer." Ty turned the boat and veered in that direction.

Austin could hardly breathe as he waited to see if this was Skye.

Alive.

It had to be Skye, alive.

He stopped himself before he considered any other options.

Austin sucked in a quick breath as the object became closer. "I think that's a person."

"I think you're right." Ty accelerated.

As they drew near, Austin realized it was definitely someone out there.

Skye. It was Skye. He was sure of it.

But she wasn't moving.

Oh, dear Jesus . . .

Ty pulled up beside her. Austin reached down and, with Wes's help, they grabbed her arms and lifted her onboard.

She wasn't breathing. And she was pale. Too pale.

Austin put his fingers to her heart. It was still beating.

Ty turned her over and began pounding on her back, trying to get the water out of her lungs.

"Come on, Skye," Austin muttered, praying she'd respond.

Ty pounded on her back again.

Austin held his breath. Waiting. Watching. Praying.

Just then, she moved. Coughed. Sputtered water.

Her eyes rushed open, and she sat up. Panic seized her as her gaze darted around wildly.

Until she saw Austin.

"Austin?"

In one move, he was beside her on the floor, and his arms wrapped around her.

Wes found a blanket and put it around their shoulders. And Austin held her, never wanting to let go. She was safe.

And he planned to keep it that way for a long time.

CHAPTER TWENTY-NINE

TWO DAYS LATER, everything was still a blur.

The good news was that Skye was safe. Nothing else suspicious had happened. And Ian was behind bars—for now. No doubt his family would do everything they could to get him out of jail. And they'd probably succeed.

But he'd already done enough damage to sideline his financial goals and maybe even his career aspirations.

Austin stepped onto the porch of his house and, from behind, wrapped his arms around Skye. She leaned into him, grateful that he was here to hold her up. Everyone needed someone like that in their lives.

"How are you?" he murmured, his breath tickling her ear.

"I'm okay. Thanks to you."

"You gave me a good scare. Please don't ever do that again."

"I have no intentions of putting myself in a situation like that again." She turned until they were face-to-face. Austin's arms remained around her, and she rested her hands on his chest, as natural as if they'd done it a million times before. "Thank you for always being there for me, Austin."

"It's been my pleasure."

She nodded toward his cottage, where he'd gone inside to take a phone call. "Who were you talking to in there?"

His breath hitched, and his gaze turned serious. "Actually, it was my mom."

Skye blinked in surprise. With everything going on, she hadn't thought to ask him about that situation. "Really? You called her?"

He nodded, emotions that Skye couldn't read etching his features. "I did. And we had a good talk."

"What did she say?"

"She mostly cried and talked about the mistake she had made in leaving me. She begged for my forgiveness."

"And?" She held her breath, waiting to hear more.

Austin shrugged. "And I forgave her."

Relief washed through Skye. Forgiveness really was possible, wasn't it? It wasn't an easy path, but it was a journey worth taking, not even for the person being forgiven but for the person doing the forgiving.

It gave her a renewed sense of hope for her future. "That's great, Austin."

Austin remained quiet a moment, and she could tell he was gathering his thoughts. She waited for him to speak.

"I've been thinking a lot lately, Skye," Austin started. "We've all made mistakes in our lives. Even my mom. But what you did . . . I would never say that putting a child up for adoption is a mistake, not when it's done for the right reasons."

She waited for him to finish.

"However, the Winthrops obviously manipulated the situation with you and forced you into a decision you weren't ready for. I'm sorry things happened that way. But I hope you'll forgive yourself."

"I'm getting there. I really am." Almost losing her life had confirmed to Skye all the resolutions and changes she'd known she needed to make. "By the way, you were the one who left that large donation at my produce stand, weren't you?"

How could she have ever thought it was Ian? Austin had been there for her the whole time, looking out for her, and taking care of her. His presence in her life was a gift— one that she never wanted to give up. She just didn't take him as the type to have disposable income. Probably because he didn't. He'd sacrificed his own needs to give her that cash. That in itself was an unforgettable gift.

He shrugged. "I don't know."

"Yes, you do. Thank you for doing that."

"I just thought those apples I was getting were very valuable."

Rising up on her tippy-toes, she planted a firm kiss on his lips—one that she hoped was the start of many to come. "You always look out for me, don't you? In fact, you knew everything I've done in my past, and you were still willing to give up your own life to save me."

"It was a no-brainer. In fact, I want to spend the rest of my life looking out for you." He dipped his head for another kiss—this one longer and deeper and swoon-worthy.

A car pulled up at that moment. She and Austin had been expecting it, but that didn't stop her nerves from flaring to life.

Skye turned from Austin, but he held her hand, as if he knew how important his support was.

Atticus Winthrop stepped out a moment later.

"I think I owe you an apology." He paused in front of her and rested his hands in his pockets. "I'm deeply sorry for my son's actions."

Skye didn't say anything.

"I think you'll be happy to know that we're not going to bail Ian out this time. He needs to learn his lesson."

"I think that's wise," Skye said. But it would take more than that for Ian to grow up.

"You still running for office?" Austin asked, his voice far from friendly.

Atticus shrugged. "I'm not sure right now. Everything is in turmoil, in case you haven't guessed. But I do have a proposal for you, Skye."

"What's that?" Skye couldn't imagine what that might be.

"If you'll keep what happened between all of us instead of going public, we can work out a deal."

"What kind of deal?" Austin said, tensing beside her, always her guardian.

"We can work out a visitation arrangement with Briar."

Skye sucked in a quick breath. "What?"

"I know you can't afford to go through the legal process to take us to court—which is what I'm assuming you're thinking about. I also know that you know that Briar is your son. There's no need to beat around the bush. However, the adoption was legal."

"I want to be a part of his life," she nearly whispered. She wanted that with every ounce of her being.

"I know you do. And I'm willing to make that happen.

All I ask for in return is that we handle this matter in a civil manner."

She shouldn't have expected anything less from the businessman.

"Where was all that civility when Briar was born and your family paid her off?" Austin snapped.

"I wasn't aware of the circumstances surrounding that at the time, but my wife has told me everything. Again, I apologize. I also apologize for what I said to you earlier this week. Skye, I've always seen something special in you. Something powerful. But I knew you could destroy what I wanted, so I tried to plant doubts in your mind. It was wrong of me."

Skye raised her chin. "I want the visitation rights to my son, but I want them with no strings attached."

"Skye . . ." Atticus's voice sounded weary.

"I don't have any desire to humiliate your family. I don't. I just want to get to know Briar. I couldn't take him away from the only parents he's known his whole life. I couldn't live with myself if I did. But I do want a relationship."

Atticus nodded slowly, almost as if defeated or like he knew better than try to compromise. "I think we can arrange that."

"I want it in writing."

He nodded, almost looking impressed for a minute. "I'll have it for you before we leave."

"I'll look for it," Skye said.

"In the meantime, I thought you might want to say hello to someone." Atticus motioned toward his car and, a moment later, Briar hopped out.

Skye felt herself grinning from ear to ear.

She released Austin's hand and went down the steps to meet the boy . . . her son. Her *son*. She still couldn't believe it.

"Hey, you." She bent down to talk to him eye to eye.

"Hi, Ms. Skye. Papa said we were coming for a visit. Is this where you live?"

She looked back at Austin's place. "No, it's my friend Austin's place."

Briar observed Austin a moment, not the least bit intimidated by him. "You're the one who saved me."

Austin smiled. "I am."

"He's really good at saving people," Skye added.

"Well, thank you."

"You're welcome, buddy."

Briar turned back to Skye. "I was hoping you might want to play sand soccer again."

"I would love to. If it's okay with your grandfather."

"Is it, Papa?" He looked back at Atticus.

Atticus hesitated before nodding. "Just have him back in three hours. Okay?"

Skye nodded. "It's a deal."

As Atticus pulled away, Austin nodded toward his house. "Let me get my keys, and I'll drive us to the beach."

Skye looked at Briar. "Could you wait here for just one minute?"

"Of course."

She followed Austin inside. As soon as the door closed, she threw her arms around him, planting a firm, long kiss on his lips.

"What was that for?" Austin asked, his voice as warm as honey when they pulled away.

"For being you. For not giving up on me."

"Never."

"You know what? I believe you—and that's a big step for me." Skye ran her finger across Austin's jaw, soaking in every inch of his face. She wanted to do that for a long time. Forever, for that matter. "I love you, Austin."

"I love you too, Skye."

ALSO BY CHRISTY BARRITT:

Hidden Currents

You can take the detective out of the investigation, but you can't take the investigator out of the detective. A notorious gang puts a bounty on Detective Cady Matthews's head after she takes down their leader, leaving her no choice but to hide until she can testify at trial. But her temporary home across the country on a remote North Carolina island isn't as peaceful as she initially thinks. Living under the new identity of Cassidy Livingston, she struggles to keep her investigative skills tucked away, especially after a body washes ashore. When local police bungle the murder investigation, she can't resist stepping in. But Cassidy is supposed to be keeping a low profile. One wrong move could lead to both her discovery and her demise. Can she bring justice to the island . . . or will the hidden currents surrounding her pull her under for good?

Flood Watch

The tide is high, and so is the danger on Lantern Beach. Still in hiding after infiltrating a dangerous gang, Cassidy Livingston just has to make it a few more months before she can testify at trial and resume her old life. But trouble keeps finding her, and Cassidy is pulled into a local investigation after a man mysteriously disappears from the island she now calls home. A recurring nightmare from her time undercover only muddies things, as does a visit from the parents of her handsome ex-Navy SEAL neighbor. When a friend's life is threatened, Cassidy must make choices that put her on the verge of blowing her cover. With a flood watch on her emotions and her life in a tangle, will Cassidy find the truth? Or will her past finally drown her?

Storm Surge

A storm is brewing hundreds of miles away, but its effects are devastating even from afar. Laid-back, loose, and light: that's Cassidy Livingston's new motto. But when a makeshift boat with a bloody cloth inside washes ashore near her oceanfront home, her detective instincts shift into gear . . . again. Seeking clues isn't the only thing on her mind—romance is heating up with next-door neighbor and former Navy SEAL Ty Chambers as well. Her heart wants the love and stability she's longed for her entire life. But her hidden identity only leads to a tidal wave of turbulence. As more answers emerge about the boat, the danger around her rises, creating a treacherous swell that threatens to reveal her past. Can Cassidy mind her own business, or will the storm surge of violence and corruption that has washed ashore on Lantern Beach leave her life in wreckage?

Dangerous Waters

Danger lurks on the horizon, leaving only two choices: find shelter or flee. Cassidy Livingston's new identity has begun to feel as comfortable as her favorite sweater. She's been tucked away on Lantern Beach for weeks, waiting to testify against a deadly gang, and is settling in to a new life she wants to last forever. When she thinks she spots someone malevolent from her past, panic swells inside her. If an enemy has found her, Cassidy won't be the only one who's a target. Everyone she's come to love will also be at risk. Dangerous waters threaten to pull her into an overpowering chasm she may never escape. Can Cassidy survive what lies ahead? Or has the tide fatally turned against her?

Perilous Riptide

Just when the current seems safer, an unseen danger emerges and threatens to destroy everything. When Cassidy Livingston finds a journal hidden deep in the recesses of her ice cream truck, her curiosity kicks into high gear. Islanders suspect that Elsa, the journal's owner, didn't die accidentally. Her final entry indicates their suspicions might be correct and that what Elsa observed on her final night may have led to her demise. Against the advice of Ty Chambers, her former Navy SEAL boyfriend, Cassidy taps into her detective skills and hunts for answers. But her search only leads to a skeletal body and trouble for both of them. As helplessness threatens to drown her, Cassidy is desperate to turn back time. Can Cassidy find what she needs to navigate the perilous situation? Or will the riptide surrounding her threaten everyone and everything Cassidy loves?

Deadly Undertow

The current's fatal pull is powerful, but so is one detective's will to live. When someone from Cassidy Livingston's past shows up on Lantern Beach and warns her of impending peril, opposing currents collide, threatening to drag her under. Running would be easy. But leaving would break her heart. Cassidy must decipher between the truth and lies, between reality and deception.

Even more importantly, she must decide whom to trust and whom to fear. Her life depends on it. As danger rises and answers surface, everything Cassidy thought she knew is tested. In order to survive, Cassidy must take drastic measures and end the battle against the ruthless gang DH-7 once and for all. But if her final mission fails, the consequences will be as deadly as the raging undertow.

YOU MIGHT ALSO ENJOY ...

THE SQUEAKY CLEAN MYSTERY SERIES

On her way to completing a degree in forensic science, Gabby St. Claire drops out of school and starts her own crime-scene cleaning business. When a routine cleaning job uncovers a murder weapon the police overlooked, she realizes that the wrong person is in jail. She also realizes that crime scene cleaning might be the perfect career for utilizing her investigative skills.

#1 Hazardous Duty

#2 Suspicious Minds

#2.5 It Came Upon a Midnight Crime (novella)

#3 Organized Grime

#4 Dirty Deeds

#5 The Scum of All Fears

When Holly Anna Paladin is given a year to live, she embraces her final days doing what she loves most—random acts of kindness. But when one of her extreme good deeds goes horribly wrong, implicating Holly in a string of murders, Holly is suddenly in a different kind of fight for her life. She knows one thing for sure: she only has a short amount of time to make a difference. And if helping the people she cares about puts her in danger, it's a risk worth taking.

THE WORST DETECTIVE EVER:

I'm not really a private detective. I just play one on TV.

Joey Darling, better known to the world as Raven Remington, detective extraordinaire, is trying to separate herself from her invincible alter ego. She played the spunky character for five years on the hit TV show *Relentless*, which catapulted her to fame and into the role of Hollywood's sweetheart. When her marriage falls apart, her finances dwindle to nothing, and her father disappears, Joey finds herself on the Outer Banks of North Carolina, trying to piece together her life away from the limelight. But as people continually mistake her for the character she played on TV, she's tasked with solving real life crimes . . . even though she's terrible at it.

ABOUT THE AUTHOR

USA Today has called Christy Barritt's books "scary, funny, passionate, and quirky."

Christy writes both mystery and romantic suspense novels that are clean with underlying messages of faith. Her books have won the Daphne du Maurier Award for Excellence in Suspense and Mystery, have been twice nominated for the Romantic Times Reviewers' Choice Award, and have finaled for both a Carol Award and Foreword Magazine's Book of the Year.

She is married to her Prince Charming, a man who thinks she's hilarious—but only when she's not trying to be. Christy is a self-proclaimed klutz, an avid music lover who's known for spontaneously bursting into song, and a road trip aficionado.

When she's not working or spending time with her family, she enjoys singing, playing the guitar, and exploring small, unsuspecting towns where people have no idea how accident-prone she is.

Find Christy online at:
www.christybarritt.com
www.facebook.com/christybarritt
www.twitter.com/cbarritt

Sign up for Christy's newsletter to get information on all of her latest releases here:
www.christybarritt.com/newsletter-sign-up/

If you enjoyed this book, please consider leaving a review.

Made in the USA
Columbia, SC
05 September 2018